CONTENTS

The Winter Promise	1
Chapter 1: The Consultant	3
Chapter 2: The First Night	10
Chapter 3: The Audit	17
Chapter 4: The First Booking	27
Chapter 5: The Workshop	39
Chapter 6: The Architect	49
Chapter 7: The Complication	61
Chapter 8: The Reckoning	71
Chapter 9: The Transformation	81
Chapter 10: The Light	92

THE WINTER PROMISE

A Villa D'Oro Novel

by

Siobhan Everleigh

Copyright © 2025 Siobhan Everleigh

All rights reserved.

No part of this book may be reproduced or transmitted in any form or by any means without written permission from the author.

This is a work of fiction. Names, characters, places, and incidents are either products of the author's imagination or used fictitiously. Any resemblance to actual persons, living or dead, or actual events is purely coincidental.

First Edition

Published by Siobhan Everleigh

CHAPTER 1: THE CONSULTANT

December 18th

Sofia Castellano had made exactly three good decisions in her life: moving back to Villa d'Oro, firing her ex-husband's lawyer before he could finish his opening statement, and never, under any circumstances, trusting a man who ordered his coffee with oat milk.

The consultant walking toward her across the piazza definitely ordered oat milk.

"Ms. Castellano?" He extended his hand—firm grip, expensive watch, the kind of smile that had closed deals in seventeen countries. British, probably London, absolutely certain he was the smartest person in any room he entered. "David Hartley. Thank you for meeting me."

"Sofia." She didn't take his hand. "And I didn't agree to meet you. You showed up."

"Your bank suggested—"

"My bank can suggest I rob a train. Doesn't mean I'm doing it." She crossed her arms, aware she was being rude and not particularly bothered by it. "You have five minutes. Talk fast."

To his credit, he didn't flinch. "Your villa is losing money. Badly. I can fix it."

"Pass."

"You haven't heard my proposal."

"Don't need to. I've met your type before—consultants who swoop in, slash everything that makes a place special, replace it with 'revenue optimization' and 'brand synergy,' then leave with a fat check while the soul bleeds out." She picked up her espresso. "Hard pass."

David Hartley did something unexpected then. He laughed.

Not the polite corporate chuckle of someone humoring a difficult client, but an actual laugh—surprised and genuine and slightly self-aware. "That's... remarkably accurate, actually."

"I know." Sofia drained her coffee. "Which is why we're done here."

"Wait." He held up a hand. "What if I told you I agree with you?"

"Then I'd say you're lying to close the deal."

"Fair." He pulled out a chair—uninvited—and sat down. Bold move. Possibly stupid. "Look. You're right. Most consultants would tell you to standardize the rooms, cut the cooking classes, fire Giulia—"

"You know Giulia's name?"

"I've done my research." He leaned forward, and his eyes were sharper than she'd expected. Darker, too. Unsettling. "I know Villa d'Oro was your grandmother's house. I know you inherited it, moved back after your divorce, that you've been running it for three years, that you're trying to create something that actually matters instead of just another cookie-cutter agriturismo. I also know that if you don't improve your occupancy rate by twenty percent in the next six months, the bank will force a sale."

Sofia's stomach went cold. "They told you that?"

"They hired me to make the problem go away." He sat back. "Question is, do you want them to make the problem go away their way, or your way?"

A couple at the next table laughed about something, the sound bright and careless. Christmas lights blinked on across the piazza, strung between buildings like captured stars.

Sofia studied him. Expensive coat, good shoes, the kind of haircut that cost more than her monthly wine budget. Everything about him screamed corporate efficiency, the exact opposite of what Villa d'Oro needed.

But his eyes didn't match the rest of him. They were tired.

"Why aren't you in London closing hostile takeovers or whatever your kind does?"

Something flickered across his face—so quick she almost missed it. "Taking a break from hostile takeovers."

"Burnout?"

"Something like that."

"And you thought Italy at Christmas was a good reset?"

"I thought working for myself instead of a firm might be." He signaled the waiter, ordered an espresso—black, no sugar, of course—and turned back to her. "Full transparency? I need this project. My reputation took a hit recently. Your villa could be a good story. 'Boutique retreat saved without losing its soul.' Makes me look less... soulless."

Sofia blinked. "Did you just admit you're using me for PR rehab?"

"Yes."

"That's either the dumbest or the smartest pitch I've ever heard."

"Let me show you which one." He pulled out his phone, slid it across the table. "These are three properties I've worked with in the last year. Small hotels, family businesses, places with actual character. I didn't gut them. I helped them find their people."

She scrolled through the photos. A coastal B&B in Cornwall. A mountain lodge in Scotland. A wine estate in Bordeaux. Before and after revenue charts that looked too good to be real, but the photos showed places that still looked... real. Imperfect. Loved.

"You did this without making them soulless?"

"That was the brief."

"From who?"

"Myself." He took his phone back. "Like I said. Trying something different."

Sofia considered this. Considered him. Considered the fact that she'd been lying awake at three a.m. for six weeks straight, running numbers that refused to add up, watching the villa she'd sacrificed her marriage to save slip through her fingers anyway.

"One month," she said. "You stay at the villa, you see how we actually operate, and then you tell me what you think. No promises, no commitments. If I like what you suggest, we talk. If not, you're gone by Epiphany."

"Deal."

"And you work. Actually work. No standing around with a clipboard looking concerned. You want to understand Villa d'Oro, you live it."

"Define 'work.'"

"Chop vegetables. Haul firewood. Set tables. Whatever Giulia tells you to do." Sofia smiled sweetly. "She doesn't like consultants either. Fair warning."

David Hartley—expensive coat, tired eyes, probably doomed—smiled back. "When do I start?"

"Now. Your car better not be blocking the fountain."

December 18th (Later)

The drive up to Villa d'Oro was every Italian cliché crammed into twelve kilometers of winding road—cypress trees, stone walls, hills the color of rust and honey. David's rental car complained on every switchback, and he was starting to suspect Sofia had given him deliberately bad directions.

Then the villa appeared, and he understood.

It wasn't grand. It wasn't polished. The terracotta walls needed repainting, the shutters didn't quite match, and the fountain in the front courtyard listed slightly to one side like it was considering retirement.

It was perfect.

Dammit.

He'd been hoping for something easy to fix—bad marketing, poor online presence, fixable inefficiencies. But this? This was the kind of place that made people cry when they left. The kind of place that ruined them for everywhere else.

The kind of place he couldn't afford to fall in love with.

A woman appeared in the doorway—silver hair, apron, the expression of someone who'd seen every type of fool and wasn't impressed by any of them.

"You're the consultant." Not a question. An accusation.

"Guilty." He got out of the car. "You must be Giulia."

"Signora Giulia. And you're late."

"Sofia told me to turn left at the—"

"Sofia lies when she thinks it's funny." Giulia wiped her hands on her apron. "Leave your bags. You're peeling potatoes."

"I'm sorry?"

"Potatoes. Peeling. Kitchen. Now." She turned and walked back inside, clearly expecting him to follow.

David looked at his car—German, efficient, already homesick for autobahns—then at the villa that smelled like woodsmoke and rosemary even from the driveway.

He'd quit a six-figure job at Deloitte for this.

"Right then." He grabbed his briefcase—still carrying it out of habit, though God knows why—and followed the terrifying Italian woman into what was probably going to be the strangest month of his life.

The kitchen was chaos. Not dirty chaos, but the warm, loud chaos of a place where actual cooking happened—copper pots hanging from hooks, herbs drying in bunches, something bubbling on the stove that smelled so good it was probably illegal.

Giulia pointed at a mountain of potatoes. "Peel. Small pieces, no eyes, don't cut yourself. I don't have time for British blood on my floor."

"Noted." He set down his briefcase, took off his coat, rolled up his sleeves.

"You know how to peel a potato?"

"I had a flat in Camden for three years. I learned or starved."

"Camden." She snorted. "That explains the sad eyes."

"I don't have sad eyes."

"All you London people have sad eyes. Like you're surprised life doesn't come with a spreadsheet." She handed him a peeler and a bowl. "Get to work. Dinner's in three hours and Emma's bringing her new boyfriend."

"Emma?"

"Long story. Pretty girl, used to be a mess, fell in love with Marco the carpenter, stayed." Giulia started chopping onions with the kind of knife work that suggested she could absolutely dismember him if needed. "Now they're adorable and we all want to vomit from happiness."

"Sounds... sweet?"

"It is. You'll hate them." She glanced at him. "Unless you're secretly a romantic, which you don't look like."

David focused very hard on peeling potatoes.

He'd been called many things in his career—ruthless, efficient, brilliant, cold. Never romantic. Not since university, anyway. Not since he'd learned that feelings were inefficient and love was just a statistical anomaly that made people make bad decisions.

The door banged open. Luigi—he'd been briefed on the dog—rocketed into the kitchen like he'd been fired from a cannon, skidded on the tiles, and crashed directly into David's legs.

"Merda," Giulia muttered. "Luigi, basta—"

But the dog was already climbing David like a furry, enthusiastic mountaineer, licking his face, his hands, the potatoes—

"Down. Down. Good God, what do they feed you—"

"Everything," said a voice from the doorway. "He eats everything. It's a problem."

David looked up.

Sofia stood in the doorway, changed out of her city clothes into jeans and a chunky sweater, her hair loose, cheeks pink from cold. She looked younger. Warmer. Real.

"Survived Giulia's interrogation?"

"Barely." He managed to extract himself from Luigi and return to the potatoes, aware he was now covered in dog hair and probably smelled like wet spaniel. "She's terrifying."

"Yes," Giulia said, not looking up from her onions. "I am."

Sofia grinned. "Welcome to Villa d'Oro, Mr. Hartley. Try not to ruin it."

CHAPTER 2: THE FIRST NIGHT

David's room was, objectively speaking, the nicest guest room at Villa d'Oro.

Which was why Sofia hated that she'd put him in it.

She should have given him the small room at the back, the one with the temperamental radiator and the view of the compost bins. Instead, some traitorous part of her brain had defaulted to hospitality mode, and now David Hartley was unpacking his precisely organized suitcase in the room with the original frescoed ceiling and the window that overlooked the valley.

Sofia stood in the hallway, arms crossed, watching him through the half-open door.

"You're lurking," Giulia said, appearing behind her with a stack of fresh towels.

"I'm supervising."

"You're lurking." Giulia pushed past her into the room. "Mr. Hartley. More towels. The good ones, because apparently Sofia has decided you deserve them."

"I didn't—"

"Thank you," David said, looking up from his laptop. He'd changed into a worn jumper that looked infinitely more comfortable than his earlier outfit, and his hair was slightly messy in a way that made him seem younger. More human. "This room is beautiful. The frescoes are eighteenth century?"

"Seventeen-ninety-two," Giulia said, warming to him immediately in the way she did with anyone who appreciated the villa's history.

"Sofia's great-great-grandmother commissioned them when she married. See the olive branches? That's the family crest."

"Remarkable." David stood, moving closer to examine the painted ceiling. "Have you considered featuring this in your marketing? Most of your online photos show the grounds, but this kind of historical detail could attract a different demographic entirely."

Sofia's jaw tightened. "We're not changing our marketing."

"I didn't say change. I said expand." He glanced at her, expression mild. "Not the same thing."

"Is there?"

"Sofia," Giulia warned.

"What? I'm just asking." Sofia leaned against the doorframe, refusing to feel guilty about her tone. "Because in my experience, consultants say 'expand' when they mean 'erase everything you've built and replace it with something more profitable.'"

David considered this. "Fair point. Though in my experience, villa owners say 'we're fine' when they mean 'I'm terrified of losing control.'"

The accuracy of this landed like a slap.

Giulia made a small noise that might have been approval, set down the towels, and left before Sofia could murder her.

"I'm not terrified," Sofia said, once they were alone.

"No?"

"No. I just don't need some stranger telling me how to run my family's property."

"Your family's property that's hemorrhaging money."

"We're doing fine."

"You're not, though." David picked up a folder from his bag—when had he printed things?—and held it out. "These are your numbers from the last three years. Occupancy rates, revenue per guest, seasonal patterns, operating costs. Do you want to look at them together, or would you prefer to keep pretending everything's fine?"

Sofia didn't take the folder. "Emma put you up to this."

"Emma asked me to help. That's not quite the same."

"She had no right—"

"She cares about you." His voice softened, just slightly. "And she's worried. Which, based on these numbers, she probably should be."

Sofia snatched the folder from his hand, flipped it open, and immediately regretted it.

Numbers. Graphs. The kind of clinical, irrefutable data that made it impossible to keep lying to herself about how bad things actually were.

"I know it's not easy to look at," David said quietly. "But ignoring it won't make it go away."

"Thank you for that profound insight." Sofia snapped the folder shut. "Anything else you'd like to explain to me about my own business?"

"Actually, yes." He crossed his arms, mirroring her posture. "Why do you hate asking for help so much?"

"I don't—"

"You do. You've been hostile since the moment I arrived, which suggests this isn't about me specifically. So what is it? Bad experience with consultants? Control issues? General distrust of men in expensive watches?"

"All of the above." Sofia tossed the folder onto his bed. "Plus you're standing in my favorite room judging my life choices."

"I'm not judging."

"You literally just handed me a folder full of evidence that I'm failing."

"No." David's voice was firm. "I handed you a folder full of evidence that you need help. Those are different things."

Sofia opened her mouth to argue, then closed it.

Because he was right, wasn't he? About the numbers, about her defensiveness, about the fact that she'd been running herself ragged for three years trying to prove she could do this alone.

God, she hated when people were right.

"Fine," she said finally. "You want to help? Start by staying out of my way."

"That's not really how consulting works."

"It's how this one works." Sofia turned to leave, then paused in the doorway. "Dinner's at seven. Don't be late, or Giulia will assume you're rude and spend the entire meal explaining why British food is an oxymoron."

"Looking forward to it," David said, and he sounded like he meant it.

Dinner was a disaster, but not in the way Sofia expected.

She'd anticipated awkward silences, David making careful observations about "market positioning," Giulia interrogating him about his intentions. What she got instead was David and Giulia bonding over their shared disdain for tourists who complained about authentic Italian coffee being "too strong," while Sofia sat at the head of the table feeling weirdly left out.

"They want it to taste like milk," Giulia was saying, gesturing with her fork. "Just milk with a whisper of coffee. An insult."

"I had a client once who asked if we could source 'gentler' beans," David said. "As if beans have emotional ranges."

"Gentler beans!" Giulia's laugh was sharp and delighted. "Americans?"

"British, actually. Surrey."

"Worse."

Sofia reached for her wine, caught David's amused glance, and felt something uncomfortable shift in her chest.

He was easy to talk to. That was the problem.

She'd expected corporate stiffness, the kind of consultant who spoke in buzzwords and never quite made eye contact. But David was... present. Engaged. He asked Giulia about her family, complimented the pasta with specific enough details that it was clear he actually understood cooking, and when Luigi dropped his head into David's lap mid-meal, he just scratched the dog's ears and kept talking.

It was disarming.

Sofia didn't trust it.

"So," she said, interrupting a conversation about the proper ratio of eggs to flour in fresh pasta. "What's your angle?"

David looked up. "Sorry?"

"Your angle. The real reason you're here." Sofia leaned forward. "Because Emma's a friend, sure, but you're a consultant. You don't work for free. So what do you get out of six weeks in rural Tuscany fixing someone else's problems?"

Giulia's fork paused halfway to her mouth.

David was quiet for a moment, and something complicated crossed his face. "Honestly?"

"Preferably."

"I needed a break." He set down his wine glass, turning it slowly between his fingers. "I've been traveling for four years straight. Different city every month, different project, different hotel room. And somewhere around Vienna last winter, I realized I couldn't remember the last time I'd stayed anywhere long enough to learn the barista's name."

"So this is a vacation."

"No. It's a test." He met her eyes. "To see if I can still do the work when I actually care about the outcome."

The honesty of this landed harder than it should have.

Sofia had built her entire defensive posture around the assumption that David was just another mercenary, here to extract value and move on. But that answer—raw and self-aware and just uncertain enough to be real—didn't fit the narrative.

"Well," Giulia said, breaking the silence. "At least you're honest. More wine?"

"Please."

The conversation moved on—Giulia telling stories about Sofia's grandmother, David asking gentle questions that showed he was actually listening. Sofia watched him from across the table, reassessing.

Maybe Emma hadn't sent her a corporate vulture.

Maybe she'd sent her someone who understood what it meant to be lost.

Later, after Giulia had gone home and the kitchen was clean, Sofia found David on the terrace.

He was standing at the railing, looking out over the valley. The December air was cold enough to see his breath, but he didn't seem to mind. Just stood there, hands in his pockets, staring at the lights of distant villages like they held answers to questions he hadn't figured out how to ask yet.

Sofia almost left him alone.

Almost.

"Can't sleep?" she asked, stepping outside.

David turned, smiled. "Too quiet. I'm used to traffic."

"You'll get used to the silence. Takes about three days."

"Is that how long it took you?"

"Longer." Sofia joined him at the railing, wrapping her cardigan tighter against the cold. "I spent the first two months convinced I'd made a catastrophic mistake. Too quiet, too isolated, too far from everything that felt like real life."

"What changed?"

"Spring came." Sofia gestured toward the dark valley. "One morning I woke up and the whole place smelled like jasmine and new grass, and I thought... oh. This is why people stay."

David was quiet, absorbing this.

"You'll feel it too," Sofia said. "The pull of this place. Fair warning."

"Is that why you're trying so hard to keep me at arm's length?" David's voice was gentle. "Afraid I'll understand why Villa d'Oro matters?"

The observation was too accurate to be comfortable.

"I'm trying to keep you at arm's length," Sofia said carefully, "because the last time I trusted someone with something I loved, they spent two years telling me I was doing it wrong."

David turned to face her fully. "Your ex-husband."

"Emma told you."

"She mentioned you were divorced. Not the details."

"Well. Now you know." Sofia crossed her arms. "So forgive me if I'm not thrilled about another man showing up with folders full of evidence that I'm failing."

"Sofia." David's voice was firm. "You're not failing. You're drowning. Those aren't the same thing."

"Feels the same from where I'm standing."

"I know." He shifted closer, not touching but present. "But here's the thing about drowning—you can't fix it alone. At some point, you have to let someone throw you a rope."

Sofia looked at him—really looked. In the dim terrace light, he seemed younger than she'd first thought. Tired in a bone-deep way that had nothing to do with jet lag and everything to do with running too long on empty.

They were both drowning, she realized.

Just in different water.

"Six weeks," she said finally.

"Sorry?"

"You get six weeks to prove Emma was right about you." Sofia met his eyes. "But if you try to turn my villa into some soulless optimization project, I'm throwing you out. Bag, laptop, expensive watch, everything."

David's smile was small but genuine. "Deal."

They shook on it, formal and slightly ridiculous, and Sofia pretended not to notice that his hand was warm despite the December cold.

Or that she held on just slightly too long before letting go.

CHAPTER 3: THE AUDIT

David started his audit at six in the morning.

Sofia knew this because Luigi woke her at six-fifteen, whining to go outside, and when she stumbled downstairs in her robe and yesterday's socks, she found David already in the kitchen with a notebook, measuring the distance between the stove and the prep counter.

"What are you doing?"

He looked up, completely unfazed by her appearance. "Morning. Measuring workflow efficiency. Your kitchen layout adds approximately twelve unnecessary steps per service."

"It's six in the morning."

"Yes." He made a note. "Did you know your largest cutting board doesn't fit in your dishwasher? You have to hand-wash it, which adds—"

"David."

"—roughly forty minutes per week to Giulia's workload, which over a year is—"

"David."

He stopped, pen hovering over paper, and seemed to actually see her for the first time. Disheveled, barely awake, holding a dog leash and radiating murderous intent.

"Too early?" he asked.

"Too early."

"Right. Coffee?"

Sofia considered throwing him out. Instead, she said, "Make it strong enough to strip paint, or don't bother."

By the time Giulia arrived at eight, David had measured every room on the ground floor, photographed seventeen "workflow inefficiencies," and reorganized Sofia's reservation system into a color-coded spreadsheet that made her actively nauseous to look at.

"This is violence," Sofia said, staring at her laptop screen.

"This is organization." David appeared beside her with fresh coffee—proper coffee, thank God, not whatever milk-adjacent beverage she'd half-expected. "See? Red is confirmed bookings, yellow is pending, green is—"

"I know what colors mean."

"Then you'll appreciate how much easier this makes capacity planning."

"I appreciate nothing before nine a.m."

"Noted." He made another note in his infernal notebook. "Also, you have three couples requesting the Emma Suite for Valentine's weekend next year."

Sofia blinked. "The what?"

"The Emma Suite. That's what guests are calling the room where Emma and Marco—" He paused, reading her expression. "You didn't know people were requesting it specifically?"

"No."

"You should lean into that." David pulled up something on his phone—of course he'd already created a digital file system—and showed her a TripAdvisor review. "Look. 'Stayed in the room where the photographer found love. Magical atmosphere. Highly recommend for romantic getaways.'"

Sofia read the review twice, something warm and complicated blooming in her chest.

Emma's room. Emma's story. Still rippling outward, bringing people here.

"We could rename it officially," David said, voice careful. "The Emma Suite. Maybe add a small plaque with the story. Not exploitative—tasteful. Just acknowledging that something special happened here."

Sofia looked at him. "That's actually a good idea."

"I have been known to have those occasionally."

"Don't let it go to your head."

"Too late." His smile was quick and unguarded, and Sofia felt that uncomfortable shift again. The one where David stopped being an obstacle and started being... something else.

Giulia burst through the door, shopping bags in both hands, and the moment shattered.

"David! You're measuring my kitchen?"

"Observing," he corrected. "Not judging."

"Everything's judging if you write it down." Giulia started unpacking vegetables with efficient violence. "Sofia, tell him to stop measuring my kitchen."

"I tried. He doesn't listen."

"Clearly." Giulia pointed a zucchini at David like a weapon. "What did you find? That I don't use enough mise en place? That my knives aren't sharp enough? That I commit crimes against workflow efficiency?"

"Actually," David said, "I found that you're doing the work of two people with the equipment budget of half a person. Your knives are impeccable, your mise en place is professional-grade, and the only crime here is that Sofia hasn't invested in proper ventilation over the stove."

Giulia stopped unpacking.

Sofia stopped breathing.

"The ventilation's fine," Sofia said.

"It's not." David pulled out his phone again—Jesus, how much documentation had he created in two hours?—and showed them a photo of the range hood. "This is residential-grade. You're running a commercial operation. Every service, smoke and heat are filling the room because this unit can't handle the volume. Giulia's working in a sauna."

"It's not that bad," Giulia said, but her voice lacked conviction.

"When was the last time you didn't leave service with a headache?"

Giulia's silence was damning.

Sofia crossed her arms. "Proper ventilation costs money we don't have."

"Proper ventilation costs less than losing Giulia to burnout." David's voice was matter-of-fact, not accusatory. "I ran the numbers. A commercial-grade hood, professionally installed, would run about four thousand euros. Your current system is costing you roughly two hundred euros monthly in wasted energy. Plus Giulia's health. Plus the guests who complain about cooking smells in the common areas."

"Guests complain about that?" Sofia looked at Giulia.

Giulia's expression said yes, she'd been protecting Sofia from that particular truth.

David continued, relentless but not cruel. "You pay it off in energy savings within two years. Faster if you factor in guest satisfaction. But the real return is keeping Giulia happy, healthy, and not secretly planning her resignation."

"I'm not—" Giulia stopped. "Okay, maybe a little bit secretly."

"Giulia!"

"What? It's hot in here! I'm fifty-three years old, Sofia. I can't work in a sauna forever."

The betrayal of this landed like a punch.

Sofia had been so focused on keeping the villa afloat that she'd missed the most obvious thing: She was sinking the person who mattered most.

"Right." Sofia's voice came out rough. "Order the hood."

"Sofia—"

"I said order it." She looked at David. "What else am I missing?"

The list, it turned out, was extensive.

They spent the rest of the morning going through David's findings, and with each new revelation, Sofia felt smaller. The towels were wrong—too thin, wrong absorbency, needed replacing. The website was a disaster—slow loading, no mobile optimization, booking system from 2015. The breakfast service was inefficient—Giulia making everything to order instead of setting up a proper buffet that would save hours of labor.

"I thought personal service was our thing," Sofia said weakly.

"It is. But personal and personalized aren't the same. Personal means you do everything; personalized means guests get exactly what they want." David pulled up photos of hotel buffets—not the sad continental ones, but beautiful Italian spreads with proper curation. "Giulia preps everything the night before, guests serve themselves, she's available for special requests but not chained to the kitchen. Everyone's happier."

"Guests want someone to make their eggs."

"Some do. Most just want good food and the option of seconds without feeling guilty." He showed her review after review citing breakfast as "lovely but slow" or "delicious but we missed our morning hike."

Sofia slumped in her chair. "This is humiliating."

"It's data."

"It's proof I've been failing for three years."

"No." David closed his laptop and looked at her directly. "It's proof you've been surviving for three years. There's a difference."

"Is there?"

"Yes." His voice was firm. "Surviving means keeping the lights on, the guests fed, the villa functioning despite impossible odds. You've done that. Alone. While grieving your marriage, rebuilding your life, and learning an entirely new industry. That's not failure, Sofia. That's extraordinary."

The kindness in this was somehow worse than criticism.

Sofia felt her throat tighten. "I should have seen it. The ventilation, the website, all of it. I should have—"

"You were too close to it." David's expression softened. "That's why outside eyes help. Not because you're incompetent, but because you're human."

Giulia, who'd been quietly prepping lunch, spoke up. "He's right, you know. You can't see everything when you're drowning in it."

"I'm not—" Sofia stopped. "Why does everyone keep saying I'm drowning?"

"Because you are, darling." Giulia's voice was gentle. "And we're all just relieved someone finally threw you a rope."

They broke for lunch—Giulia's ribollita, thick with beans and yesterday's bread, the kind of soup that felt like being hugged from the inside. David ate two bowls and complimented the seasoning with specific enough detail that Giulia actually blushed.

"You know food," she said approvingly.

"My mother was a chef. Restaurant in Leeds." David mopped his bowl with bread. "She'd have loved this. The beans are perfect—not mushy."

"Good breeding, your mother."

"Terrifying woman, actually. She once made a sous chef cry for oversalting béarnaise."

"I like her already."

Sofia watched them banter, feeling oddly outside the moment. David fit here. That was the unsettling part. He measured and analyzed and optimized, yes, but he also appreciated the soup. Understood why Giulia's cooking mattered. Saw the difference between efficiency and soul.

Maybe Emma had been right to send him.

Maybe Sofia had been wrong to resist so hard.

"Okay," she said, interrupting a debate about the proper ratio of bread to tomatoes in pappa al pomodoro. "What's the total damage?"

David pulled out his notebook. "For essential upgrades—ventilation, website overhaul, new towels, some minor equipment—you're looking at roughly twelve thousand euros."

Sofia's stomach dropped. "I don't have twelve thousand euros."

"I know. That's why I prioritized." He showed her a new list, this one color-coded. "Green is critical—do immediately. Yellow is important—do within six months. Red is aspirational—do when you're profitable. We focus on green first."

"Which is?"

"Ventilation and website. Everything else can wait."

"That's still six thousand euros."

"Yes." David leaned forward. "But here's the thing. You're undercharging."

"What?"

"Your rates are too low. You're competing on price when you should be competing on experience." He pulled up a comparison chart—of course he had a comparison chart. "Similar properties in this region charge thirty to forty percent more for comparable accommodations. You could raise your rates tomorrow and still be competitive."

"People won't pay more."

"The right people will." His voice was certain. "You're not trying to attract bargain hunters. You're trying to attract the guests who value what you offer—authenticity, history, Giulia's cooking, the whole Villa d'Oro experience. Those people will pay premium rates. Happily."

Sofia stared at the numbers, her brain struggling to reorganize three years of assumptions.

"How much should I charge?"

"For the Emma Suite during high season? Four hundred euros per night."

"That's insane."

"That's market rate for a boutique property with your amenities and story." He showed her comparable listings. "Look. Same region, similar size, less charm. All charging more."

"But what if no one books?"

"Then we adjust. But Sofia—" He waited until she looked at him. "You have to stop undervaluing yourself. The villa, yes, but also you. Your taste, your vision, the experience you've created. It's worth more than you're charging."

The words landed somewhere deeper than business advice.

Sofia had spent three years trying to prove she could do this. Three years running herself ragged, keeping prices low, saying yes to every guest, bending over backward to prove she deserved to be here.

And maybe—just maybe—she'd been proving it to the wrong person.

"Four hundred euros," she said quietly.

"For the Emma Suite. We'll adjust other rooms proportionally."

"And if it doesn't work?"

"Then we try something else." David's smile was reassuring. "But it will work."

Giulia set down a plate of biscotti, patted Sofia's shoulder, and said nothing. Sometimes silence was the most eloquent support.

That evening, Sofia updated the website herself.

David had offered to help, but she needed to do this alone. Needed to type the new numbers, write the new descriptions, claim the new value she'd been too afraid to ask for.

The Emma Suite: €400/night. Where one story ended and another began.

Her hand hovered over the "publish" button.

Three years of undercharging. Three years of believing she had to earn her place here through martyrdom and discount rates.

Three years of being told she was too much, so she'd tried to be less.

Sofia clicked publish.

The world didn't end.

She sat back, staring at her laptop, waiting for the panic to hit. Instead, she felt something unexpected:

Relief.

A knock on her office door. David, holding two glasses of wine.

"Saw the light on. Figured you could use this."

"You figured right." Sofia accepted the glass. "I did it. New rates. Live as of now."

"How does it feel?"

"Terrifying. Liberating. Like jumping off something tall." She took a long drink. "Ask me again in a week when no one books."

"Someone will book." David settled into the chair across from her desk. "Probably by tomorrow."

"You don't know that."

"I do, actually. Your villa has a ninety-two percent occupancy rate from repeat guests and referrals. Those people aren't price-sensitive. They're experience-sensitive. They'll pay more because they know what they're getting."

Sofia wanted to argue, but the logic was sound.

"You're very certain about things," she said instead.

"Comes with the job."

"Is it exhausting? Being that certain?"

David's smile faded slightly. "Sometimes. Especially when I'm not certain at all."

"And when is that?"

He was quiet for a moment, turning his wine glass slowly. "More often than you'd think."

The admission hung between them, honest and unexpected.

Sofia studied him in the dim office light. He looked tired—not physically, but in that deeper way that came from carrying too much for too long. She recognized it because she saw the same thing in her mirror every morning.

"Why did you really come here, David?"

"I told you. I needed—"

"The real reason."

He met her eyes, and something shifted. Some decision made.

"My ex-wife told me I was never actually present," he said quietly. "That I was always analyzing, optimizing, solving problems instead of just... being with her. Being anywhere, really." He looked down at his wine. "She wasn't wrong. I spent fifteen years perfecting the art of being professionally present while being emotionally absent. And then one day she was gone, and I realized I'd never actually learned how to just exist in a place."

"So this is practice."

"This is a test." He looked up. "To see if I can still feel something. Anything. Before I'm completely hollowed out."

The raw honesty of it stole Sofia's breath.

She'd been so focused on protecting herself from him that she hadn't seen he was just as wounded. Just as afraid.

"For what it's worth," she said carefully, "you seem pretty present to me."

"Do I?"

"Yeah. You noticed Giulia was burning out. You noticed the guests requesting Emma's room. You noticed I was drowning before I admitted it to myself." Sofia leaned forward. "That's not analysis, David. That's care."

Something complicated crossed his face. Hope, maybe. Or the memory of hope.

"Thank you," he said quietly.

They sat in comfortable silence, drinking wine, not needing to fill the space with words.

Outside, the December wind picked up, rattling the windows. Inside, something between them settled. Not romance—not yet—but recognition.

Two people who'd been running for too long, finally standing still.

CHAPTER 4: THE FIRST BOOKING

The booking came through at 2:47 a.m.

Sofia knew this because she was awake, staring at her ceiling, mentally catastrophizing about the new rates. She heard the email ping on her phone, ignored it for three minutes while imagining it was a cancellation, then finally checked.

Emma Suite - February 14-16 €1,200 total

Sofia sat up so fast she startled Luigi, who'd been sleeping across her feet.

Someone had just paid twelve hundred euros.

For two nights.

In her villa.

She read the booking confirmation three times, convinced it was a mistake or a glitch or some kind of cosmic prank. But no—there it was. A couple from Milan. Anniversary trip. Special requests: champagne on arrival, roses in the room, breakfast in bed both mornings.

Sofia scrambled out of bed, padded down the hallway in bare feet, and knocked on David's door before her brain caught up with the terrible idea this was.

No answer.

She knocked again, harder.

"David."

A pause, then movement. The door opened to reveal David in pajama bottoms and a t-shirt, hair completely disheveled, squinting at her like she might be a hallucination.

"What's wrong? Is there a fire?"

"Someone booked."

"What?"

"Someone booked the Emma Suite. Valentine's weekend. Twelve hundred euros." Sofia shoved her phone at him. "Look."

David took the phone, read the screen, and smiled—slow and genuine and maybe a little smug.

"Told you."

"You told me someone would book. You didn't say it would happen in six hours."

"Markets respond quickly to proper pricing." He handed back her phone, leaning against the doorframe. "Congratulations. You just made your first premium sale."

Sofia stared at the confirmation email, something warm and unfamiliar blooming in her chest.

Pride, maybe.

Or hope.

"They want champagne," she said.

"So get champagne."

"And roses."

"Also gettable."

"And breakfast in bed both mornings, which means Giulia will have to—" Sofia stopped, looked up at David. "Why are you smiling like that?"

"Because you're already planning how to deliver an exceptional experience instead of panicking about the price." His expression softened. "That's the difference between surviving and thriving, Sofia. You just crossed it."

The compliment landed somewhere tender.

Sofia had spent so long believing she was failing that success felt foreign. Suspicious. Like something that would evaporate if she looked at it too hard.

"I woke you up," she said, suddenly aware she was standing in his doorway at three in the morning in her pajamas.

"You did."

"Sorry."

"Don't be." David's voice was warm. "This is good news. Worth losing sleep over."

They stood there for a moment, the hallway dark except for the light spilling from his room. He looked different without his usual polish—younger, more uncertain, touchingly rumpled.

Human, Sofia thought. He looks human.

"Go back to bed," David said gently. "You can celebrate properly in the morning."

"Right. Yes. Bed." Sofia backed away, clutching her phone like evidence. "Thank you. For the rates thing. For being right."

"Anytime."

She made it three steps before turning back. "David?"

He hadn't closed the door yet. "Yeah?"

"You're present right now. In case you were wondering."

His smile was small but real. "Good to know."

By morning, there were two more bookings.

Sofia discovered this over coffee—proper coffee, made by David, who'd apparently claimed the kitchen as his base of operations and was now creating some kind of complex breakfast spread.

"You're cooking," Sofia said, stopping in the doorway.

"I'm experimenting. There's a difference." He gestured to the counter, which held eggs, cream, herbs, and what looked like fresh ricotta. "Giulia's buffet concept got me thinking about breakfast optimization. What if we offered a signature dish? Something Instagram-worthy that guests would specifically request?"

"You want to make breakfast Instagramable."

"I want to make breakfast memorable." He cracked eggs with practiced efficiency. "Every successful boutique property has a signature offering. Yours could be Giulia's baking, but that's already well-known. What about a seasonal specialty? Something that changes monthly, showcases local ingredients, gives guests a reason to return?"

Sofia watched him cook—confident, methodical, clearly enjoying himself.

"You really were raised by a chef."

"She'd kill me for using this much cream." He whisked something golden and aromatic. "But yes. Food was love in our house. Still is, when I'm home. Which isn't often."

"When was the last time?"

David paused, thinking. "Christmas. Two years ago."

"David."

"I know." He poured the egg mixture into a hot pan, watching it shimmer. "I'm working on it. The being present thing. Turns out it requires actually being places."

Sofia perched on the counter—Giulia would kill her—and studied him. "Is that what this is? Practice?"

"Maybe." He added herbs, ricotta, tilted the pan with casual expertise. "Or maybe it's just nice to cook for someone who isn't paying by the hour."

The omelet he produced three minutes later was, objectively, perfect. Golden, fluffy, folded with the kind of precision that came from years of practice. He plated it, added a small salad, drizzled something that smelled like heaven, and presented it to Sofia.

"Your signature breakfast."

She took a bite and actually made a noise.

"Oh, that's unfair."

"Good?"

"That's restaurant quality." Sofia took another bite, trying to identify the flavors. Lemon? Thyme? Some kind of magic? "Giulia's going to hire you."

"I'm already employed, thanks." But he looked pleased, in that quiet way of people who rarely let themselves enjoy compliments.

The kitchen door banged open and Giulia arrived, arms full of groceries, freezing mid-step when she saw David at the stove.

"What is this?"

"David made breakfast," Sofia said around another bite. "It's obscene. Try it."

Giulia set down her groceries, accepted a fork, tasted the omelet, and went very still.

"You learned this from your mother?"

"And about three years in Lyon, yes."

"Lyon." Giulia made a thoughtful noise. "This is French technique with Italian heart."

"Is that a compliment?"

"It's an observation." But Giulia took another bite. And another. "What's the cream ratio?"

"Two-to-one eggs to cream, but the secret is—"

"Temperature. I know." Giulia pointed her fork at him. "You're dangerous."

"I get that a lot."

"I mean for Sofia's wallet." Giulia's eyes gleamed. "If we put this on the menu, people will pay extra just for breakfast."

"That's the idea."

Sofia watched them talk through variations—seasonal ingredients, presentation options, whether tourists would pay fifteen euros for a premium breakfast experience. Their conversation was rapid-fire, technical, the kind of shorthand that came from shared understanding.

David fit here.

The realization was becoming harder to ignore.

They spent the morning planning the Valentine's booking.

Giulia had opinions about the roses (local only, no grocery store garbage), the champagne (prosecco, not French, this was Italy for

God's sake), and the breakfast menu (David's omelet, plus her orange almond cake, plus fresh-pressed juice from the grove).

"The couple wants romance," Giulia declared. "We give them romance. Italian romance. Not whatever sanitized hotel version they're expecting."

"What's Italian romance?" David asked, taking notes.

"Abundance. Beauty. The feeling that someone cared enough to make everything perfect." Giulia gestured broadly. "We don't do minimal. We do maximal. With taste."

"Maximal with taste," David repeated, writing this down. "Got it."

Sofia watched them work, something settling in her chest. This. This was what she'd been trying to build. Not just accommodation, but experience. Not just service, but care.

She'd been so focused on survival that she'd forgotten the vision.

"What about music?" Sofia asked suddenly.

They both looked at her.

"For Valentine's dinner. Most couples will go to town, but what if we offered a private dinner here? Terrace, if the weather holds. Giulia cooks, we set up fairy lights, maybe find someone local to play guitar?"

Giulia's face lit up. "Marco knows a musician. Plays classical Italian songs. Very romantic."

"We could offer it as an add-on," David said, already calculating. "Premium romantic dinner package. Three courses, wine pairing, musician, sunset terrace. Charge—what—two hundred euros per couple?"

"Two-fifty," Sofia countered.

David grinned. "Look at you. Embracing premium pricing."

"Don't get cocky." But Sofia was smiling. "Can we actually pull this off?"

"We can pull this off," Giulia said firmly. "David, you handle the logistics. I'll handle the menu. Sofia—"

"I'll handle the romance part." Sofia pulled out her phone. "I know exactly who to call."

Emma answered on the second ring.

"Sofia! Is everything okay?"

"Everything's perfect. How do you make someone fall in love with a place?"

A pause. "That's a very specific question for ten in the morning."

"I have a Valentine's couple coming. I want to destroy them with romance." Sofia paced the terrace, her mind already spinning. "You did travel writing. You know what makes experiences memorable. What's the secret?"

"Honestly?" Emma's voice softened. "It's the small things. The details no one expects. At Villa d'Oro, it was the figs. Finding them in the garden, eating them straight from the tree, feeling like I'd discovered something secret."

"Figs in February are impossible."

"So find your February equivalent. What's magical about Villa d'Oro in winter?"

Sofia looked out at the valley—bare vines, silver olive trees, morning mist clinging to the hills.

"The quiet," she said slowly. "Summer's all activity and abundance. But winter is... intimate. Like the villa's keeping secrets just for you."

"There you go. Lean into that." Emma paused. "Is this David's doing? The sudden business strategy?"

"Partially."

"And?"

"And what?"

"Sofia." Emma's voice carried that particular friend-telepathy that saw through evasions. "You called me at ten in the morning about creating romance. You never call before noon. What's happening?"

Sofia sighed. "He's good at his job."

"That's not what I asked."

"He's also..." Sofia searched for words. "Present. Competent. Makes perfect omelets. Understands why things matter instead of just analyzing them. Giulia likes him, which is basically unheard of. And he looks at me like I'm capable instead of chaotic."

"Oh," Emma said softly. "Oh, Sofia."

"It's not like that."

"What's it like?"

"It's..." Sofia stopped. What was it like? "Confusing. I hired him to fix my business, not to make me reconsider my entire stance on trusting people."

"Those aren't mutually exclusive."

"They should be."

"Why?" Emma's voice was gentle. "Sofia, I know your ex did a number on you. But David isn't him. And more importantly—you're not the same person you were in that marriage."

The truth of this landed hard.

Sofia had spent three years defining herself against her ex-husband's criticisms. Too loud. Too much. Too chaotic. She'd built Villa d'Oro as proof she could succeed despite being all those things.

But what if she'd been asking the wrong question?

What if the problem wasn't that she was too much—but that he'd been too little?

"I have to go," Sofia said. "Guest preparations."

"Sofia—"

"Thank you. For the advice. And for sending him."

"I didn't send him to fix your business," Emma said quietly.

"I know."

David found her an hour later, surrounded by fabric samples and sketches.

"What's all this?"

"Romance." Sofia gestured to her planning chaos. "Emma said it's about unexpected details. So I'm creating unexpected details."

He picked up a sketch—her terrible drawing of the terrace with fairy lights, flowers, candles. "This is ambitious."

"This is February fourteenth. If we're charging two thousand euros for a weekend, we deliver magic."

"Fair point." David sat down beside her, studying her notes. "Talk me through your vision."

"Okay." Sofia pulled out her concept list. "They arrive. Champagne, yes, but in the garden, not the room. We set up a small table by the olive grove, bundle them in blankets, let them watch the sunset with prosecco and Giulia's almond biscuits. First impression: this place is special."

"Good start."

"Dinner—private, terrace, Marco's musician friend playing. Three courses, all Tuscan, wine from the local vineyard. Giulia makes her chocolate torta for dessert because it's basically edible seduction."

"Noted."

"Breakfast in bed both mornings—your omelet, Giulia's orange cake, fresh juice, roses on the tray. Then on their last morning, we pack them a picnic. They can hike to the ridge, eat lunch overlooking the valley, leave feeling like they discovered something secret."

David was quiet for a moment, reading through her notes.

"This is really good, Sofia."

"Yeah?"

"Yeah." He looked at her, expression serious. "You're not just planning an experience. You're planning a memory. That's the difference between service and hospitality. You understand that instinctively."

The compliment hit differently than the business ones. This felt personal. Seen.

"My grandmother used to say that," Sofia said quietly. "That hospitality was about creating memories, not just comfort. I'd forgotten that. Got so focused on survival that I stopped thinking about magic."

"Well, you're remembering now." David's smile was warm. "And if this couple doesn't fall in love with Villa d'Oro—and possibly each other all over again—I'll eat my notebook."

Sofia laughed, surprised by how easy it felt. "That's a terrible bet."

"I stand by it."

They worked through the afternoon, refining details, making lists, arguing good-naturedly about candle placement and whether the prosecco should be served in flutes or coupes. The planning felt less like work and more like collaboration. Creation.

Fun, Sofia realized. This was actually fun.

She'd spent so long being terrified that she'd forgotten what it felt like to enjoy building something.

That evening, Giulia left early—something about her sister's birthday—and Sofia found herself alone in the kitchen with David, preparing dinner.

"I can cook," she protested when he started chopping vegetables.

"I know you can. But this is faster with two people." He handed her a knife. "You dice the onions. I'll handle the tomatoes."

"Bossy."

"Efficient."

They fell into rhythm—companionable silence punctuated by the sounds of chopping, the kitchen warm and aromatic. David moved around the space with easy confidence, and Sofia realized she'd stopped watching him like a threat and started watching him like... something else.

"Can I ask you something?" David said, not looking up from his cutting board.

"Depends on the question."

"Why did you really buy Villa d'Oro?"

Sofia's knife paused. "That's a big question for dinner prep."

"I know. But I'm curious. You gave up everything—your life in Rome, your marriage, financial security. Most people don't make those kinds of leaps without a powerful reason."

"What makes you think I had a reason beyond stubbornness?"

"Because stubborn people dig in. Brave people leap." He glanced at her. "You leaped."

Sofia set down her knife, considering her answer.

"I spent fifteen years trying to be the right size," she said finally. "Quieter. Calmer. More palatable. And one day I woke up and realized I'd made myself so small that I'd disappeared entirely. The villa was my grandmother's favorite place. She was loud, chaotic, unapologetically herself. Being here felt like permission to take up space again."

David had stopped chopping, giving her his full attention.

"And did it work?"

"I don't know yet." Sofia smiled, but it was uncertain. "I'm still figuring out how much space I'm allowed to take."

"Sofia." David's voice was firm. "You're allowed to take all the space you want."

"Am I?"

"Yes." He moved closer—not touching, but present. "Your ex-husband was wrong. You're not too much. You're exactly the right amount of Sofia. And anyone who can't handle that doesn't deserve you."

The words landed somewhere she hadn't known was empty.

Sofia looked at him—really looked. At some point in the last four days, David Hartley had stopped being an intruder and become something else entirely. An ally. A mirror. Someone who saw her clearly and didn't flinch.

"Thank you," she said quietly.

"You're welcome."

They stood there in the kitchen, dinner half-prepped, something shifting between them. Not romance—not yet—but possibility.

The beginning of recognition that this thing between them might be more than professional.

Outside, the December sun slipped toward the horizon, painting the valley in shades of gold and amber.

Inside, something new was beginning to grow.

CHAPTER 5: THE WORKSHOP

David disappeared for three days.

Not literally—Sofia saw him at breakfast, caught glimpses of him measuring things or typing on his laptop in the library. But he stopped asking questions. Stopped presenting findings. Just observed, made notes, and vanished into whatever corner of the villa he'd claimed as his temporary office.

It was unnerving.

Sofia had gotten used to his constant presence, his questions, his spreadsheets. The silence felt like waiting for a diagnosis you knew would be bad.

On the fourth morning, he found her in the garden, pruning olive trees with more aggression than the task required.

"I have a proposal," he said.

Sofia didn't look up. "Does it involve firing Giulia or painting everything beige?"

"Neither. Can you put down the shears before I explain? You're making me nervous."

She set them down. "Talk."

David pulled out his phone—always the phone, always the data—and showed her a document. "I've spent three days analyzing your operation. The good news: Villa d'Oro has exceptional bones. The guest experience is authentic, the setting is unmatched, and your word-of-mouth reputation is stellar."

"I feel a 'but' coming."

"But you're operating at about sixty percent capacity. You have the demand—people want to come here. You just can't accommodate them with your current infrastructure."

"Infrastructure." Sofia crossed her arms. "You mean money."

"I mean smart investment." He swiped to a new screen. "Your biggest constraint is rooms. You have six guest accommodations. During high season, you turn away three bookings for every one you accept. That's leaving roughly forty thousand euros on the table annually."

The number made Sofia's stomach clench.

"So your solution is what—build more rooms? I don't have that kind of capital."

"You don't need to build. You need to convert." David gestured toward the far end of the property. "Marco's workshop. It's the size of a small house, barely used for actual carpentry anymore, and it has those massive doors that could be incredible as windows. Convert it into a luxury suite—one room, but premium. Charge double your current rate."

Sofia stared at him. "You want me to kick Marco out of his workshop?"

"I want you to ask Marco if he'd consider it. Asking isn't demanding."

"He'll say no."

"Then we find another solution." David's voice was patient. "But Sofia, you can't keep running this place on charm and stubbornness alone. At some point, you have to grow or you'll fold."

The truth of this landed hard.

Sofia looked toward the workshop—a stone building half-covered in vines, its weathered doors always slightly ajar. Marco had been using it since before she'd moved back, storing tools and building furniture and generally treating it like his personal refuge from villa chaos.

Asking him to give it up felt impossible.

But losing Villa d'Oro felt worse.

"I'll talk to him," she said quietly.

Marco was, predictably, in the workshop.

Sofia found him sanding a table—long, rustic, the kind of piece that would anchor a room and make everything else feel temporary by comparison. He looked up when she entered, reading her expression immediately.

"You're about to ask me something I won't like."

"How do you know?"

"You're doing the thing with your hands." He gestured. "The twisting thing. You only do that when you're nervous."

Sofia stopped twisting her hands. "David has a proposal."

"David's full of proposals."

"This one involves your workshop."

Marco set down his sanding block, giving her his full attention. "I'm listening."

Sofia explained—haltingly, apologetically—about the capacity problem, the lost revenue, David's idea to convert the workshop into a premium guest suite. Marco listened without interrupting, his expression unreadable.

When she finished, he was quiet for a long moment.

"You need the money," he said finally.

"I need to keep the villa."

"Same thing." He ran his hand over the table's surface, testing for smoothness. "When would this happen?"

"Marco, I'm not—you can say no. I'm just asking."

"I know." He smiled, but it was complicated. "And I'm asking when. Because if it needs to happen, it needs to happen."

Sofia felt her throat tighten. "You've been here longer than I have. This space is yours."

"The villa is yours. I'm just borrowing corner space." He gestured around the workshop—tools hanging on walls, half-finished projects stacked against windows, sawdust coating every surface.

"Besides, I've been meaning to clean this place for years. You're giving me a deadline."

"You don't have to be noble about this."

"I'm not being noble. I'm being practical." Marco picked up his sanding block again, but didn't use it. "Your grandmother would want you to do whatever it takes to keep this place alive. Even if it means kicking out her favorite carpenter."

"You were her favorite?"

"Obviously. I'm everyone's favorite." His smile was more genuine now. "Talk to David. Figure out the timeline. I'll start moving my things."

Sofia crossed to him, pulled him into a hug before he could protest. "Thank you."

"Don't thank me yet. Wait until you see how much of my stuff I try to relocate to the villa's common areas." He hugged her back, solid and reassuring. "It'll be fine, Sofia. Change is just the villa evolving."

"When did you become wise?"

"I've always been wise. You just don't listen."

She pulled back, laughed despite the tightness in her chest. "Where will you work?"

"I'll figure it out. Maybe build something smaller. Or work outside when weather permits." He shrugged. "I'm adaptable. It's my best quality."

"I thought your best quality was making furniture."

"That's my second-best quality."

David was waiting in the courtyard when Sofia returned, pretending to read something on his phone but clearly watching for her.

"Well?"

"He said yes."

David's relief was visible. "Really?"

"Really. Though I think he's planning to passive-aggressively store lumber in the library as revenge."

"I'll take it." David made a note—of course he made a note. "We should get an architect out here. Someone local who understands historic buildings. The conversion needs to be done right—preserving the character while modernizing functionality."

"You know an architect?"

"I know three. I'll make calls." He looked at her, expression softening. "This is good, Sofia. You're making the right choice."

"It doesn't feel right. It feels like displacement."

"It feels like growth. There's always discomfort in growth."

"Very philosophical for a consultant."

"I contain multitudes." His smile was warm. "Come on. Let's walk through the workshop together. I want to show you what I'm seeing."

The workshop was bigger than Sofia remembered.

She'd been in here dozens of times, but always focused on Marco or whatever he was building. Now, seeing it through David's eyes—through the lens of possibility rather than habit—the space transformed.

"Look at this." David gestured to the massive doors. "These could be floor-to-ceiling glass. Sliding, so they open completely in summer. The view from here is spectacular."

Sofia followed his gaze. He was right—the workshop faced southwest, overlooking the valley and distant villages. With proper windows, it would be flooded with light.

"The bones are excellent," David continued, running his hand along the stone wall. "Original construction, probably same era as the main villa. We preserve the stone, add modern amenities—luxury bathroom, proper heating—but keep the rustic character. Exposed beams, the original floors."

"It'll be expensive."

"It'll pay for itself in two years. Less, if we market it right."

He pulled out his phone, showed her comparison listings. "Look. Similar properties with luxury suites charge premium rates. We position this as the Villa d'Oro Artisan Suite—exclusive, limited availability, perfect for couples who want privacy within community."

Sofia walked the space, imagining it. A bed where Marco's workbench stood. A bathroom where tools were stacked. Guests drinking morning coffee where she'd watched Marco sand furniture for hours.

It felt like erasure and evolution in the same breath.

"What if it doesn't work?" she asked quietly.

"Then we tried something." David moved beside her, close but not touching. "But Sofia—it will work. I've done this before. I know what's possible."

"You're very certain."

"Only about data. The rest is faith." He smiled. "Luckily, you have enough faith for both of us."

"Do I?"

"You moved back here after your divorce. Started a business with no formal training. Kept it running through three years of barely breaking even. You're either faithful or insane."

"Can't I be both?"

"Absolutely." His expression turned serious. "But for what it's worth, I think what you've built here is extraordinary. Not despite the challenges, but because of them. You didn't take the easy path. You took the meaningful one."

The compliment landed somewhere tender.

Sofia had spent so long defending her choices—to her ex-husband, to her family, to herself—that she'd forgotten what it felt like to have someone simply see the value without needing to be convinced.

"Thank you," she said quietly.

"You're welcome."

They stood in the workshop's fading light, the space full of possibility and memory in equal measure. Outside, Luigi barked at something. Giulia's voice carried from the kitchen, singing off-key in Italian.

The villa hummed with life, as it always did.

David's phone buzzed. He glanced at it, then looked back at Sofia. "The architect I mentioned—she's available to visit next week. Should I set it up?"

Sofia took a breath. This was it. The moment where intention became action. Where possibility became commitment.

"Yes," she said. "Set it up."

David smiled—genuine and warm and maybe slightly proud. "Good choice."

"We'll see." But Sofia was smiling too, despite her nerves. "Fair warning: if this goes badly, I'm blaming you."

"Fair warning: if this goes well, I'm taking credit."

"Deal."

That evening, Sofia found herself on the terrace again—her thinking spot, apparently. The December air was sharp and clean, stars beginning to emerge in the darkening sky.

She heard footsteps behind her. David, carrying two glasses of wine.

"You're making this a habit," she said.

"I'm providing moral support. There's a difference." He handed her a glass, settled against the railing beside her. "How are you feeling about the workshop decision?"

"Terrified. Excited. Guilty. Hopeful." Sofia took a long drink. "Is it possible to feel all of those at once?"

"It's called growth. Very uncomfortable. Highly recommend it."

She laughed despite herself. "You're annoyingly optimistic."

"Only about other people's businesses. My own life is a disaster."

"Is it?"

David was quiet for a moment, turning his wine glass slowly. "I've spent four years perfecting the art of professional competence while avoiding anything that requires actual emotional investment. So yes. Disaster."

"That seems like a harsh assessment."

"It's an accurate one." He looked at her, and his expression was unusually open. "I can optimize businesses, improve systems, maximize revenue. But I can't seem to figure out how to just... exist. Without analyzing everything to death."

"Maybe that's not a flaw. Maybe that's just who you are."

"My ex-wife would disagree."

"Your ex-wife sounds like she wanted you to be someone else."

"Maybe. Or maybe she just wanted me to be present." He set down his glass. "I'm trying to learn how. It's harder than it should be."

Sofia studied him in the dim light. "You seem pretty present to me."

"Do I?"

"Yeah. You notice things. You listen. You see what's actually happening instead of just what you want to see." She paused. "That's not analysis, David. That's attention. It's a completely different thing."

Something shifted in his expression—surprise, maybe, or recognition.

"Thank you," he said quietly.

"You're welcome."

They stood in comfortable silence, drinking wine, watching stars emerge one by one. The villa glowed behind them, warm and welcoming. Somewhere inside, Giulia was banging pots with characteristic violence.

"Can I ask you something?" David said.

"Depends on the question."

"Why did your marriage end?"

Sofia tensed, then forced herself to relax. Fair question. She'd asked about his divorce. "He told me I was too much."

"Too much what?"

"Just too much. Too loud. Too emotional. Too Italian." She smiled, but it was hollow. "He loved me at first—said my passion was infectious. But over time, it became exhausting instead of charming. So I tried to be less. Quieter. Calmer. More manageable."

"Did it work?"

"For a while. Then he left anyway, said he didn't recognize me anymore." Sofia laughed, sharp and bitter. "The irony is I'd changed entirely for him, and he left because I'd changed."

"He's an idiot."

"He's remarried. To someone very quiet and serene."

"Still an idiot." David's voice was firm. "Sofia, you're not too much. You're exactly the right amount. And anyone who can't handle that is the problem, not you."

She'd heard this before—from Emma, from Giulia, from well-meaning friends who didn't understand that knowing something intellectually and believing it emotionally were completely different things.

But hearing it from David felt different.

Maybe because he'd seen her at her most defensive, most chaotic, most authentically herself. And he hadn't flinched. Hadn't tried to manage her or tone her down or suggest she be more reasonable.

He'd just... met her where she was.

"Thank you," she said, and meant it.

"Anytime."

The moment stretched between them—not quite romantic, but intimate in a way that felt significant. Like something was shifting, settling into place.

David's phone buzzed. He checked it, grimaced. "The architect. She can come Monday."

"That's fast."

"She's local and curious. Apparently she's been wanting to see inside Villa d'Oro for years but never had an excuse."

"Well, now she has one."

"Now she has one." David pocketed his phone, looked at Sofia. "You're doing the right thing. I know it doesn't feel like it, but you are."

"How do you know?"

"Because you're choosing the villa's future over your own comfort. That's not a small thing."

Sofia finished her wine, set the glass down on the terrace wall. "For what it's worth, I'm glad Emma sent you."

"Yeah?"

"Yeah. Even though you're annoying and overly organized and you measure things at six in the morning."

"High praise."

"Don't let it go to your head."

He smiled—warm and genuine and maybe slightly smug. "Too late."

They stood there a moment longer, the December night settling around them, the villa warm at their backs. Something had shifted tonight. Not dramatically, but definitely. The space between them felt different. Smaller, maybe. Or just more intentional.

Sofia wasn't sure what it meant.

But for the first time in years, she wasn't afraid to find out.

CHAPTER 6: THE ARCHITECT

The architect arrived Monday morning in a battered Vespa and a cloud of enthusiasm that made Sofia instantly exhausted.

"Sofia! Finally!" The woman—late fifties, silver hair in a wild bun, wearing what appeared to be vintage Pucci—kissed both her cheeks before Sofia could prepare herself. "I'm Francesca. I've been dying to see this place for twenty years. Your grandmother once told me I had terrible taste in men but excellent taste in buildings. She was right about both."

"You knew my grandmother?"

"Everyone knew Lucia. She was impossible to miss." Francesca was already moving toward the workshop, her enthusiasm a force of nature. "David! You didn't lie. This is spectacular."

David emerged from the workshop, looking amused. "I never lie about architecture."

"You lie about everything else, though."

"Frequently."

Sofia watched them banter, feeling oddly outside the moment. Francesca had that immediate intimacy some people possessed—like she'd known you forever and was simply resuming a conversation interrupted yesterday.

"Sofia, come." Francesca beckoned imperiously. "Tell me everything. What's the vision? What are you trying to create?"

"I—" Sofia struggled to articulate something she'd only half-formed. "Something that feels authentic. Not like a hotel trying to be rustic, but actually... real."

"Good. Real is harder than fake, which is why most people choose fake." Francesca circled the workshop, running her hands along walls, testing door hinges, examining beams with the focused attention of someone who actually saw structure instead of space. "This building is 1680s. Same era as the main villa. Beautiful bones. Criminal that it's been used for storage."

"It's been used for carpentry," Marco said mildly, appearing from behind a stack of lumber.

Francesca whirled. "And you are?"

"Marco. The carpenter being evicted."

"Ah. The sacrifice." Francesca studied him with unnerving intensity. "You built the pergola, yes? And the gates? I noticed them on the way in."

"I did."

"Excellent work. Clean lines, respectful of the original structure." She turned back to the workshop. "When do you vacate?"

"When Sofia needs me to."

"Next week, then. I'll need the space empty to do proper measurements." Francesca pulled out a tablet—apparently even wild creative spirits had gone digital—and started making notes. "David, you mentioned preserving character while modernizing. What's the budget?"

"Flexible," David said carefully.

"That means limited. I understand." Francesca moved to the massive doors, pushing one open to frame the valley view. "These stay. We reinforce them, add glass panels, make them operable. The stone walls stay. The beams stay. Everything original that can be preserved, we preserve."

"And the modern parts?" Sofia asked.

"Hidden. Bathroom tucked behind a partition that looks like it's always been there. Heating under the floors. Smart lighting that mimics candles. The guests should feel like they're staying in a converted artisan workshop, not a hotel room cosplaying as one."

Despite herself, Sofia was drawn in. "How long would this take?"

"Six weeks if we're lucky. Eight if we're realistic. Twelve if Marco's spirits haunt the construction crew." Francesca grinned at Marco. "No offense."

"None taken. I plan to haunt aggressively."

"Good man." Francesca made more notes, muttering to herself in Italian that Sofia only half-caught. Something about load-bearing walls and plumbing nightmares and the tragedy of modern building codes.

David moved beside Sofia, voice low. "What do you think?"

"I think she's terrifying."

"She's brilliant. Also terrifying. But mostly brilliant."

"How do you know her?"

"I consulted on a hotel project in Siena three years ago. She was the architect. We argued for two months straight, then became friends once I admitted she was right about everything."

"You admitted you were wrong?"

"It happens. Occasionally. Under duress."

Francesca called from across the workshop. "Sofia! Come look at this."

Sofia joined her at the far wall, where Francesca was examining what looked like old water damage.

"See this?" Francesca traced the staining. "This wall is slightly damp. There's a drainage issue outside—probably been there for decades. We fix it during construction, or you'll have mold problems within a year."

"That sounds expensive."

"Less expensive than rebuilding the wall later." Francesca's voice was matter-of-fact. "David said your budget is flexible, which means tight. I can work with tight. But I won't work with willful ignorance. We do it right, or we don't do it."

Sofia appreciated the bluntness. "Okay. What else needs fixing?"

"Everything and nothing." Francesca gestured broadly. "The structure is sound. The problems are all cosmetic or systems-related. Which means they're fixable, just annoying." She turned to David. "I'll need three days to do a full assessment. Drawings, cost estimates, timeline. Then we meet, discuss, decide."

"Perfect," David said.

"I'll also need access to the main villa. If I'm designing for Villa d'Oro, I need to understand Villa d'Oro." Francesca looked at Sofia. "Can you give me a tour? The real tour, not the guest version."

"Now?"

"Why not?"

The tour took two hours.

Francesca wanted to see everything—guest rooms, kitchen, storage areas, the attic Sofia had forgotten existed. She asked questions constantly, made notes furiously, and had opinions about things Sofia had never considered.

"This light fixture is wrong for the space."

"That doorway was widened at some point—see the newer stonework?"

"Your grandmother had excellent taste in tile. Terrible taste in curtains."

By the time they finished, Sofia felt like she'd been through an audit and a therapy session simultaneously.

They ended in the courtyard, Francesca accepting coffee from Giulia with the ease of someone who'd done this a thousand times.

"Your villa is remarkable," Francesca said, settling at the table. "Not perfect—perfect is boring. But authentic. It feels lived in. Loved."

"It is loved," Sofia said quietly.

"Good. That matters." Francesca sipped her coffee, made an appreciative noise. "This is perfect espresso. You must be Giulia."

"I am."

"Lucia told me you were the real genius here. She was correct." Francesca set down her cup. "Sofia, can I be honest with you?"

"I'd prefer it."

"The workshop conversion is a good idea. Smart business, preserves the building, creates new revenue. David's instincts are solid." She leaned forward. "But don't let it consume you. The villa's charm is that it's not trying too hard. The moment you start optimizing everything, you lose what makes this place special."

"I'm not trying to optimize everything."

"Not yet. But David is a consultant. Optimization is his religion." Francesca's smile was knowing. "He's good at his job. Just remember—you're good at yours, too. Don't let him erase what you've built while improving it."

The observation landed uncomfortably.

Sofia had been so focused on survival that she hadn't considered this angle. What if David's improvements made Villa d'Oro more profitable but less itself?

"How do I balance that?"

"You already know how. You've been doing it for three years." Francesca stood, gathering her things. "Trust your instincts, Sofia. They've kept you alive this long. They'll keep you alive through construction, too."

After Francesca left—a whirlwind departure involving air-kisses and promises to return Thursday—Sofia found David in the library, typing furiously on his laptop.

"She's intense," Sofia said.

"She's perfect for this project." David looked up. "What did you think?"

"I think she's right about the drainage issue. And probably right about everything else."

"Usually is." He closed his laptop. "She seemed to like you."

"She seemed to like the villa. I'm not sure she has opinions about me yet."

"Give her time. She'll develop extremely specific opinions, then share them whether you want them or not."

Sofia sat in the chair across from him. "Can I ask you something?"

"Always."

"Are we going to ruin this place trying to save it?"

David was quiet for a moment, taking the question seriously. "That's the risk with any improvement project. You change too much, you lose what made it special in the first place."

"So how do we avoid that?"

"You don't let me make decisions alone." His voice was firm. "Every choice, we discuss. You have veto power over anything that feels wrong. I'm here to provide options and expertise, but this is your villa. Your vision. I'm just helping you achieve it."

"You say that now. But what if we disagree?"

"Then we disagree. And we figure it out." He leaned forward. "Sofia, I'm not here to colonize Villa d'Oro with corporate strategy. I'm here to help you build something sustainable without losing what makes it yours. The moment I forget that, you remind me. Loudly, if necessary."

"I can do loud."

"I've noticed."

They smiled at each other—easy and warm and slightly conspiratorial.

The library was quiet around them, afternoon light slanting through windows, dust motes drifting lazily through golden air. Somewhere in the kitchen, Giulia was singing again. Luigi's tags jingled as he investigated something outside.

The villa hummed with ordinary life.

"Thank you," Sofia said quietly.

"For what?"

"For taking this seriously. For seeing what matters." She gestured vaguely. "I know I've been difficult. Defensive. I just—"

"You've been protecting something you love. That's not difficult, Sofia. That's brave."

The compliment settled somewhere warm.

They sat in comfortable silence for a moment, and Sofia found herself studying him. The way afternoon light caught in his hair. The slight crease between his eyebrows when he was thinking. The competent hands that were always holding a phone or notebook but looked surprisingly gentle at rest.

When had David stopped being an intrusion and become part of the landscape?

She couldn't pinpoint the exact moment. It had happened gradually—like seasons changing, barely noticeable until suddenly everything was different.

"I should let you work," Sofia said, standing.

"You're not interrupting."

"Still." She moved toward the door, paused. "David?"

"Yeah?"

"I'm glad you're here."

His smile was soft and genuine. "Me too."

That evening, Marco found Sofia in the workshop.

She'd been avoiding it since Francesca's visit—some superstitious part of her brain worried that spending time here would make the conversion feel more real, more final. But eventually guilt won, and she came to help Marco pack.

"You don't have to do this," Marco said, carefully wrapping chisels in cloth.

"I know. But I want to." Sofia picked up a box of nails, unsure where to put it. "Where's all this going?"

"Storage shed for now. Some of it to my apartment. The rest—" He shrugged. "I'll figure it out."

They worked in companionable silence for a while, the familiar rhythm of sorting and packing. The workshop felt different already—emptier, more like a space waiting to become something else.

"I'm sorry," Sofia said quietly.

"Don't be. This is good for the villa."

"It's not good for you."

"It's not bad for me either." Marco set down a box, looked at her seriously. "Sofia, I knew when I started using this space that it wasn't permanent. Buildings at Villa d'Oro serve the villa first, my convenience second. That's how it should be."

"Still feels wrong."

"Wrong is letting the villa fail because we're too sentimental to change." He smiled. "Your grandmother would kick both our asses for overthinking this."

"She probably would."

"Definitely would." Marco returned to packing. "Besides, this gives me an excuse to build a new workshop. Smaller, better organized, maybe with actual ventilation instead of opening doors and hoping."

"You're being very gracious about this."

"I'm being practical. There's a difference." He picked up a hand plane—old, well-used, probably his favorite tool. "This place has given me a lot. Given me purpose after Emma and I didn't work out. Given me community. Given me a reason to stay in one place instead of drifting. The least I can do is give it this one room back when it needs it."

Sofia felt her throat tighten. "When did you get so wise?"

"I've always been wise. You just don't notice because you're too busy catastrophizing."

"I don't catastrophize."

"Sofia. You catastrophize breathing."

She laughed despite herself. "Fair point."

They continued packing as twilight settled over the valley. Through the workshop's open doors, Sofia could see lights beginning to glow in distant villages. The December air smelled like wood smoke and coming cold.

"Do you think we're doing the right thing?" she asked.

Marco didn't answer immediately. When he did, his voice was thoughtful. "I think you're doing the necessary thing. Whether it's right or wrong doesn't matter as much as whether it works."

"Very philosophical."

"I contain multitudes." He grinned. "Also, David's rubbing off on me. I caught myself talking about 'workflow optimization' yesterday. It was deeply disturbing."

"He is rather infectious."

"Is he?" Marco's tone was carefully neutral, but Sofia caught the edge of curiosity.

"What?"

"Nothing. Just—you seem lighter lately. Happier. I wasn't sure if it was the business improvements or the consultant himself."

Sofia felt heat rise to her face. "It's the business improvements."

"If you say so."

"I do say so."

"Mm-hmm." Marco returned to his packing, but she could see him smiling.

"He's here to help with the villa," Sofia insisted. "That's all."

"Sure. That's why you're blushing."

"I'm not blushing."

"You're absolutely blushing."

"Marco—"

"It's fine, Sofia. I'm just observing." He looked up, expression gentler. "For what it's worth, I like him. He's good for you. Good for the villa. Good for everyone, really, except possibly Giulia's sense of kitchen ownership."

"Nothing's happening between us."

"Yet."

"Marco."

"What? I'm just saying—if something did happen, hypothetically, I wouldn't disapprove. Neither would Emma. Or Giulia, though she'd pretend to be scandalized."

Sofia threw a wadded cloth at him. "You're impossible."

"I'm supportive. There's a difference."

Later, Sofia found herself on the terrace again—apparently this was her designated processing spot now. The December night was cold enough to see her breath, stars sharp and bright overhead.

She heard footsteps, already knew who it would be.

David appeared with two glasses of wine. "You're going to freeze out here."

"I'm Italian. We don't feel cold."

"That's medically improbable." He handed her a glass anyway, settled beside her at the railing. "How was packing?"

"Sad. Necessary. Marco's being impossibly gracious about the whole thing."

"He seems like a good person."

"The best." Sofia sipped her wine. "He also thinks something's happening between us."

The words were out before she could stop them.

David was very still. "Does he?"

"Apparently we're either very obvious or he's very perceptive."

"Probably both." David's voice was careful. "Is he right?"

Sofia's heart kicked against her ribs. "I don't know. Is he?"

"That depends."

"On?"

"On whether you want him to be right."

The question hung between them—direct and terrifying and impossible to evade.

Sofia looked at David—really looked. At some point in the last two weeks, he'd stopped being the consultant she resented and become someone she looked for. Someone whose presence made ordinary moments feel significant. Someone who saw her clearly and hadn't left.

"I think," she said slowly, "that I'm scared of wanting him to be right."

"Why scared?"

"Because the last time I wanted something this much, it ended with someone telling me I was too much to love long-term." She looked away. "And you're leaving in four weeks. And I'm not sure I can handle wanting something temporary."

David set down his wine glass, turned to face her fully.

"Sofia, look at me."

She did.

"I'm not your ex-husband. I'm not going to love you and then decide you're exhausting. I'm not going to make you small to make myself comfortable." His voice was firm, certain. "And I don't know what happens in four weeks. Maybe I leave and this was just a nice moment. Maybe I stay. Maybe we figure something out. But right now—right here—I'm not thinking about leaving. I'm thinking about how much I want to kiss you."

Sofia's breath caught.

"So the question isn't whether something's happening between us," David continued. "The question is whether you want it to happen. Because I do. Very much. But only if you do too."

The honesty of it was devastating.

Sofia had spent three years protecting herself from wanting. Three years convincing herself that safety was better than possibility. Three years believing that the right person wouldn't come, so why bother hoping?

But here was David. Present and honest and looking at her like she was exactly right instead of too much.

And Sofia was so tired of being afraid.

"I want it to happen," she said quietly.

"Yeah?"

"Yeah."

David smiled—slow and warm and slightly relieved. "Good."

He moved closer, giving her time to change her mind, time to step back. But Sofia didn't step back. She stepped forward, closing the distance between them.

When he kissed her, it was gentle and certain in equal measure. Not tentative, but not demanding. Just present. Just real.

Sofia felt something in her chest unlock.

She kissed him back, her hands finding the front of his shirt, holding on. He tasted like wine and possibility. His hands cupped her face, thumbs stroking her cheekbones, and for once Sofia didn't feel like too much.

She felt like exactly enough.

When they pulled apart, David rested his forehead against hers.

"That was—"

"Yeah," Sofia agreed.

"Are you okay?"

"Better than okay." She laughed, surprised by her own certainty. "I'm really good, actually."

"Good." He kissed her again, briefer but no less meaningful. "For the record, I've been wanting to do that for at least a week."

"Only a week?"

"I'm slow to catch on."

"Clearly."

They stood together in the December cold, wrapped in the warmth of discovery. The villa glowed behind them, windows golden with light. Inside, Giulia was probably preparing dinner, Marco was probably finishing his packing, Luigi was probably destroying something expensive.

Life continued, ordinary and extraordinary in the same breath.

But out here, on the terrace, something new had begun.

CHAPTER 7: THE COMPLICATION

Christmas arrived at Villa d'Oro the way it always did—gradually, then all at once.

Sofia woke to find Giulia had invaded the courtyard overnight, transforming it into something from a Italian grandmother's fever dream. Garlands of pine and cypress draped every surface. Candles clustered in terracotta pots. A nativity scene occupied the fountain, complete with hand-painted figurines that had probably been in Giulia's family since the Renaissance.

"When did you do all this?" Sofia asked, finding Giulia arranging yet another candle grouping.

"This morning. Four a.m. Couldn't sleep."

"Because?"

"Because Christmas waits for no one, and this courtyard was looking sad." Giulia stepped back, assessing her work with a critical eye. "Better. Still needs more candles."

"There are approximately four hundred candles already."

"Four hundred and twelve. And we need six hundred minimum for proper ambiance."

"That seems excessive."

"That seems Italian." Giulia pointed at her. "You're helping me hang lights this afternoon. No arguments."

"I wasn't going to argue."

"Yes, you were. You always argue about decorations. 'Too much, Giulia.' 'People will think we're trying too hard, Giulia.'" She waved dismissively. "This year, we're trying exactly hard enough. David agrees with me."

"David has opinions about Christmas decorations?"

"David has opinions about everything. Apparently it's a professional requirement." Giulia's smile was knowing. "Also, he was asking where you keep the ladder. I told him the tall one is unstable and he should absolutely not use it alone."

"Which means he's definitely using it alone."

"Obviously. Men never listen." Giulia returned to her candle arranging. "Go save him from himself. I have six hundred candles to place."

Sofia found David in the library, balanced precariously on the unstable ladder, trying to hang garland above the bookshelves.

"Giulia said not to use that ladder."

"Giulia says many things." David didn't look down, focused on securing a particularly stubborn pine branch. "Most of them accurate. This ladder is genuinely terrible."

"Then why are you using it?"

"Because the library needed garland and I have opposable thumbs." He finally looked down, smiled when he saw her. "Morning."

"Morning." Sofia's chest did something complicated at the sight of him—rumpled sweater, concentration face, completely at ease in her grandmother's library like he'd always belonged there. "You don't have to decorate."

"I want to. Besides, Giulia's in full Christmas mode. Resistance is futile."

"This is true."

David secured the last bit of garland, climbed down carefully. The ladder wobbled ominously. He stepped off just as it threatened to collapse entirely, catching it before it could damage anything.

"See? Perfectly safe."

"You have an interesting definition of safe."

"I have an interesting definition of many things." He moved

closer, and Sofia's breath caught slightly. They hadn't been alone since the kiss three days ago—both of them busy with villa preparations, guests arriving, Francesca's constant architectural demands. "Hi."

"Hi."

"I've been trying to get you alone for seventy-two hours."

"I've noticed."

"And?"

"And I've also been trying to get you alone for seventy-two hours." Sofia smiled. "Apparently running a villa during Christmas is incompatible with new romance."

"We should fix that."

"Should we?"

David's answer was to kiss her—gentle and certain and somehow more intimate than their first kiss. Sofia leaned into it, her hands finding his shoulders, holding on.

When they pulled apart, he was smiling.

"I've been wanting to do that since Tuesday."

"Only Tuesday?"

"I'm being conservative. The actual number is closer to constantly."

Sofia laughed, surprised by how easy this felt. How uncomplicated, despite everything. "Giulia knows."

"Of course she does. Giulia knows everything."

"She's pretending not to notice."

"That's her gift to us. Plausible deniability." David tucked a strand of hair behind her ear. "Are you okay with this? With us?"

"I think so." Sofia considered. "I'm terrified, obviously. But also... happy. Which is confusing."

"Terror and happiness aren't mutually exclusive."

"Apparently not." She kissed him again, brief but meaningful. "We should probably help Giulia before she stages a candle intervention."

"Probably."

Neither of them moved.

"David?"

"Yeah?"

"I'm really glad you're here."

His smile was soft and genuine. "Me too."

The afternoon disappeared into Christmas preparations.

Sofia and David hung lights—hundreds of them—while Giulia directed from below like a conductor leading an orchestra. Marco appeared mid-afternoon with fresh pine garlands and extremely specific opinions about placement. Even Luigi contributed, though his contribution mostly involved stealing ribbon and hiding it in places they'd find months later.

By evening, Villa d'Oro glowed.

The courtyard was transformed—lights strung overhead creating a canopy of gold, candles clustered on every surface, pine and cypress filling the air with their sharp, clean scent. The nativity scene presided over the fountain like benevolent royalty. Even the villa itself seemed to glow differently, warm and welcoming in a way that went beyond mere electricity.

"It's perfect," Sofia said quietly, standing in the courtyard's center.

"It's excessive," Giulia corrected. "Which makes it perfect."

They'd invited the Valentine's couple—Alessandro and Francesca (different Francesca, which caused immediate confusion)—to join them for dinner. The couple had arrived that afternoon, and Sofia had watched them fall in love with Villa d'Oro in real-time. The way Alessandro's hand found his wife's. The way Francesca's eyes filled when she saw their room. The way they both went quiet on the terrace, overwhelmed by the valley view.

This. This was why the villa mattered.

Dinner was chaotic and lovely—Giulia's five-course menu, local wine, conversation flowing in Italian and English and the occasional confused mixture of both. Alessandro was a professor,

Francesca a librarian. They'd been married twenty years, weathered rough patches, were here to remember why they'd chosen each other.

"We almost didn't make it," Francesca confided to Sofia over dessert. Alessandro was deep in conversation with David about something academic and incomprehensible. "Two years ago, we nearly divorced. Just... drifted apart. Forgot why we liked each other."

"What changed?"

"We remembered that liking someone is a choice you make daily." Francesca's smile was complicated. "Marriage isn't the big moments. It's choosing to stay interested in someone's boring stories. To laugh at their terrible jokes. To keep seeing them clearly even when familiarity makes them invisible."

Sofia felt something catch in her chest.

She glanced at David, caught him already looking at her. He smiled—small and private and just for her.

"That's wise," Sofia said quietly.

"That's survival." Francesca raised her wine glass. "To Villa d'Oro. For reminding us what we almost forgot."

They toasted—to the villa, to memory, to the persistence of love despite everything working against it.

Later, after Alessandro and Francesca had retreated to their room, the four of them sat in the courtyard—Sofia, David, Giulia, and Marco. The candles burned low. The December air was cold but not bitter.

"This was good," Marco said quietly.

"This was perfect," Giulia corrected.

"Do you ever just accept compliments without editing them?" Marco asked.

"No. Where's the fun in that?"

They bickered comfortably while Sofia and David sat in companionable silence. His hand found hers under the table—casual, comfortable, like they'd been doing this for years instead of days.

Sofia's phone buzzed. She almost ignored it, but something made her check.

An email. Subject line: "Villa d'Oro - Media Inquiry."

She opened it, skimmed quickly, felt her stomach drop.

"What's wrong?" David asked quietly.

"It's from a travel journalist. British publication—fairly big. They want to feature Villa d'Oro in their 'Hidden Gems of Tuscany' series." Sofia looked up. "They want to come in January. Stay for a week. Interview me, photograph everything, write a major feature."

"Sofia, that's incredible," Marco said.

"That's terrifying."

"That's marketing gold," David added, but his voice was careful. "What's the concern?"

Sofia stared at the email, her mind racing. This was good news. Obviously good news. The kind of exposure that could transform Villa d'Oro from struggling property to destination.

But.

"They want to feature the 'authentic Italian villa experience,'" she read aloud. "Intimate, family-run, unchanged by modern commercialization." She looked at David. "We're literally in the middle of commercializing. The workshop conversion, the rate increases, all of it."

"You're not commercializing," David said firmly. "You're professionalizing. That's not the same—" He stopped himself. "That's not what they're asking you to give up."

But Sofia heard the uncertainty.

Because what if he was wrong? What if the moment they finished the workshop conversion and implemented all of David's improvements, Villa d'Oro stopped being the authentic gem this journalist wanted to feature?

What if they were destroying the thing that made them special?

"I need to think about this," Sofia said quietly.

She stood, needing space, needing air. David's hand slipped from hers as she moved away from the table.

"Sofia—" he started.

"I just need a minute."

She walked to the edge of the courtyard, looked out at the valley. Behind her, she heard Giulia say something quiet to David. Marco's response. The sound of chairs moving.

Her phone buzzed again. Another email.

This one from her bank.

She opened it, already knowing it would be bad.

It was worse.

The loan payment she'd deferred—the one buying her time to implement David's changes—was coming due in six weeks. Early February. And the amount was larger than she'd remembered. Much larger.

Sofia did quick math in her head. Even with the Valentine's booking, even with raised rates, even with everything going perfectly...

She might not make it.

The workshop conversion would take eight weeks minimum. The journalist wanted to visit in January, before construction finished. If the feature ran and brought new bookings, she wouldn't have capacity to accommodate them until March at earliest.

Everything was timing out wrong.

She felt David's presence before he spoke.

"Talk to me."

"The bank payment is due February fifteenth." Her voice was flat. "Thirty-two thousand euros."

David was quiet for a moment. "That's... significant."

"That's impossible." Sofia turned to face him. "Even with everything we're doing, I won't have it. The workshop won't be generating revenue yet. I'll have construction costs instead of income. I'm going to lose the villa, David."

"No, you're not."

"The math doesn't work."

"Then we change the math." His voice was firm, certain. "We accelerate the workshop timeline. Push Francesca to finish in six weeks instead of eight. Open it Valentine's weekend with premium pricing—call it a 'preview rate' if it's not completely finished."

"That's insane."

"That's adaptive." He pulled out his phone—always the phone, always the solutions. "We can do this, Sofia. The journalist visit actually helps. You offer them the workshop as exclusive access, charge them premium rate plus media exposure value. That's another twelve hundred euros. We maximize every booking between now and February—"

"David, stop."

He stopped, looking at her.

"This is exactly what Francesca warned me about," Sofia said quietly. "Optimizing everything until the soul bleeds out. We're trying so hard to save Villa d'Oro that we're killing what makes it worth saving."

"That's not what's happening."

"Isn't it? We're rushing construction, maximizing bookings, calculating media exposure value. Where's the space for anything authentic? Where's the part where this place is about memory instead of revenue?"

"Sofia, you can have both—"

"Can I? Because right now it feels like I'm choosing between survival and soul. And I don't know how to do both."

The words hung between them, sharp and true.

David's expression was complicated—frustrated, sympathetic, maybe slightly hurt. "So what do you want to do?"

"I don't know." Sofia felt tears threatening. "Maybe... maybe I should just sell. Let someone else deal with it. Someone who doesn't care if it becomes just another boutique property with no history and perfect Instagram lighting."

"You don't mean that."

"Don't I?" She laughed, hollow. "David, I'm exhausted. I've been fighting for three years to keep this place alive, and I'm losing. Maybe that's the universe telling me to let go."

"Or maybe," David said carefully, "the universe is telling you to accept help instead of martyring yourself."

The observation landed like a slap.

"That's not fair."

"Isn't it? You're so committed to doing this alone that you'd rather fail than succeed with support." His voice wasn't cruel, just honest. "Sofia, I'm trying to help you. Let me help you."

"By turning Villa d'Oro into an optimization project? By calculating everything, maximizing everything, stripping away anything that doesn't generate revenue?"

"That's not what I'm doing—"

"That's exactly what you're doing!" Sofia's voice rose. "That's what you do, David. You analyze and improve and make things efficient. But some things shouldn't be efficient. Some things should be messy and chaotic and slightly impractical because that's what makes them real."

"So you'd rather lose the villa than compromise?"

"I'd rather lose the villa than lose myself saving it."

The silence that followed was devastating.

David looked at her—really looked—and Sofia saw the moment he understood. This wasn't about the villa anymore. This was about her. About the years she'd spent making herself smaller, more manageable, more acceptable. About the marriage she'd sacrificed herself to save.

She'd come back to Villa d'Oro to reclaim her space. And now she was doing it again—shrinking to fit someone else's vision.

Even if that someone was trying to help.

"I need to be alone," Sofia said quietly.

"Sofia—"

"Please."

David nodded, stepping back. His expression was carefully neutral, but Sofia saw the hurt beneath it.

He walked away, back toward the villa, leaving her alone in the courtyard with six hundred candles and a choice she didn't know how to make.

Behind her, Giulia appeared.

"That was painful to watch."

"You were listening?"

"Everyone was listening. You were yelling." Giulia settled beside her on the fountain's edge. "You want my opinion?"

"Not particularly."

"You're getting it anyway." Giulia was quiet for a moment. "Your grandmother used to say that the villa tests everyone who loves it. Tests whether they love the idea of it or the reality of it. Whether they'll fight for it or just admire it from a distance."

"What's your point?"

"My point is David's fighting for it. And you're fighting him instead of fighting with him." Giulia stood, patting Sofia's shoulder. "Figure out which battle you're actually in, darling. Because right now you're losing both."

She left, taking her wisdom and her candles with her.

Sofia sat alone in the courtyard, surrounded by Christmas beauty and impossible choices.

The villa glowed around her, warm and welcoming and possibly slipping through her fingers.

And for the first time in three years, Sofia wondered if love was enough to save something.

Or if sometimes, despite everything, you still had to let go.

CHAPTER 8: THE RECKONING

Sofia didn't sleep.

She spent the night in her office, staring at spreadsheets that refused to add up no matter how many times she recalculated. The bank payment. The construction costs. The timeline. The journalist. The Valentine's booking that suddenly felt like a bandaid on a hemorrhage.

By dawn, she'd made a decision.

She was going to sell.

Not immediately. Not dramatically. But she'd contact a real estate agent, get the villa appraised, start the process. Maybe she'd find a buyer who'd keep it running as a retreat. Maybe not. Either way, she'd be free.

The thought should have brought relief.

Instead, it felt like grief.

Sofia made coffee—strong, bitter, the kind that tasted like punishment—and took it to the terrace. The December morning was cold and clear, frost coating the olive trees in silver. The valley stretched below, villages still sleeping, smoke beginning to rise from distant chimneys.

Beautiful. Always beautiful.

She'd miss this.

"You're up early."

Sofia turned. Emma stood in the terrace doorway, wrapped in a blanket, hair messy from sleep.

"Emma? What are you doing here?"

"Marco called. Said you were having a crisis and refusing to be reasonable about it." Emma moved to join her at the railing. "So I drove over. Marco makes excellent crisis coffee, by the way."

"It's six in the morning."

"Crisis doesn't care about time zones." Emma studied her face. "You look terrible."

"Thank you."

"I mean it affectionately." Emma accepted the coffee Sofia handed her. "Talk to me. What's happening?"

Sofia explained—haltingly, exhaustedly—about the bank payment, the timing crisis, David's solutions, their argument. Emma listened without interrupting, her expression shifting from concern to understanding to something that looked suspiciously like frustration.

When Sofia finished, Emma was quiet for a long moment.

"So your solution is to give up."

"My solution is to accept reality."

"No." Emma's voice was firm. "Your solution is to run before anyone can see you fail. Which is what you've always done, Sofia."

The observation stung.

"That's not fair."

"Isn't it?" Emma turned to face her fully. "You ran from Rome when your marriage ended. You ran back here instead of fighting for what you'd built. And now you're running again because things are hard and you're scared."

"I'm not scared—"

"You're terrified. Of needing help. Of being vulnerable. Of letting someone see you struggle and still choosing to stay." Emma's expression softened. "Sofia, David isn't your ex-husband. He's not trying to make you smaller. He's trying to help you grow."

"By turning my villa into a business optimization project?"

"By giving you tools to save something you love." Emma set down her coffee. "You know what I see when I look at what's happening here? I see someone who loves you enough to fight for your dream when you're too tired to fight for it yourself. That's not control, Sofia. That's partnership."

Sofia felt her throat tighten. "What if he's wrong? What if all these changes destroy what makes Villa d'Oro special?"

"What if they don't? What if they give you the breathing room to actually enjoy this place instead of drowning in it?" Emma moved closer. "You're so afraid of losing the villa's soul that you're willing to lose the villa entirely. That's not protection, that's self-sabotage."

The words landed like a verdict.

Because Emma was right. Sofia had spent three years claiming she was fighting for the villa when really she was fighting to prove she didn't need anyone. That she could do this alone. That needing help meant weakness.

But maybe weakness and wisdom weren't mutually exclusive.

Maybe asking for help was the bravest thing she could do.

"I yelled at him," Sofia said quietly.

"So apologize."

"I told him he was destroying everything that matters."

"So take it back." Emma's smile was gentle. "Sofia, the beautiful thing about words is you can always say different ones. Better ones. Truer ones."

"What if he doesn't want to hear them?"

"Then he's not the man I think he is. But I don't believe that." Emma squeezed her hand. "Go talk to him. Figure this out together. That's what partners do."

Sofia found David in the workshop.

He was measuring something—always measuring, always analyzing—but stopped when he heard her footsteps.

"Hi," she said.

"Hi." His voice was carefully neutral.

"Can we talk?"

"If you want to."

The formality hurt. But Sofia deserved it.

She moved further into the workshop, the space already transforming. Marco had cleared most of his tools. Francesca had left architectural drawings pinned to a makeshift board. The massive doors were propped open, framing the valley view in cold morning light.

"I'm sorry," Sofia said quietly.

David set down his measuring tape. "For what specifically?"

"For yelling. For accusing you of destroying the villa. For making you the villain when you're trying to help." She took a breath. "For being so scared of losing myself that I pushed you away instead of letting you in."

He was quiet for a moment, watching her.

"I'm not your ex-husband, Sofia."

"I know."

"I'm not trying to make you smaller or more manageable."

"I know that too. Intellectually. But emotionally..." Sofia gestured helplessly. "I spent five years in a marriage where every part of myself that was too loud or too much got slowly edited away. And I came back here determined never to shrink again. Never to compromise. Never to need anyone."

"That's not strength. That's isolation."

"I'm learning that." She moved closer. "David, you were right. I'd rather fail alone than succeed with help. Because failure feels like my fault, but success with help feels like... like proof I'm not enough on my own."

"You're enough on your own. But you don't have to be on your own." His voice softened. "Sofia, partnership isn't about proving you don't need anyone. It's about choosing to build something together that's better than what either of you could build alone."

The simplicity of this hit hard.

Sofia had been so focused on independence that she'd forgotten interdependence was an option. That needing someone didn't mean weakness. That accepting help didn't mean surrender.

"I want to try," she said quietly. "Not selling. Not giving up. Actually trying. With you."

David's expression shifted—relief and something deeper.

"Yeah?"

"Yeah." Sofia closed the distance between them. "But I need you to understand—I can't lose the villa's soul saving its body. The moment this place stops being real, it stops being worth saving."

"I understand that."

"Do you? Because you're a consultant, David. Optimization is your instinct. But not everything should be optimized."

"I know." He took her hands, holding them gently. "Sofia, I don't want to turn Villa d'Oro into another cookie-cutter property. I want to give you the tools to keep it exactly what it is—authentic, chaotic, yours—while also making it sustainable. Those things aren't mutually exclusive."

"Aren't they?"

"No. Look at what we've already done. The rate increase—that's not selling out, that's valuing what you offer appropriately. The workshop conversion—that's not commercialization, that's smart use of space. The systems Giulia uses now—that's not optimization stripping away character, that's giving her time to focus on the cooking that makes this place special."

Sofia hadn't thought of it that way.

She'd been so focused on what might be lost that she hadn't noticed what was being protected.

"You really believe this can work?"

"I know it can work." David's certainty was steady, grounding. "But only if you let me help you. Really help you. Not just implement solutions while you fight me every step."

"I'm not good at accepting help."

"I've noticed. Luckily, I'm very persistent."

Sofia laughed despite herself. "That's one word for it."

"What's another?"

"Stubborn. Annoying. Slightly arrogant about data."

"All accurate." He pulled her closer. "But also here. And not leaving. Even when you yell at me in courtyards."

"Especially when I yell at you in courtyards?"

"Especially then."

They stood in the workshop's cold morning light, holding each other, the valley stretching below them in shades of silver and gold.

"I don't know how to do this," Sofia admitted quietly. "The partnership thing. The asking for help thing. I'm going to be terrible at it."

"Probably. But I'm terrible at being present, and you've been patient with that."

"Have I?"

"Occasionally. When you're not yelling."

She laughed, burying her face in his chest. He smelled like coffee and cold air and possibility.

"We're a disaster," she said.

"We're a work in progress. Not the same thing."

Sofia pulled back, looked at him. "You did it again."

"Did what?"

"Made a distinction. You can't help yourself."

"It's my love language. Accept me for who I am."

"Fine. But only because you make good coffee."

"I'll take it." David kissed her forehead. "So. We're trying this? Actually trying?"

"We're trying this." Sofia took a breath. "Which means I need to respond to the journalist. And contact Francesca about accelerating the timeline. And figure out how to make thirty-two thousand euros materialize out of thin air."

"Not thin air. Strategic planning." David pulled out his phone—of course. "I have ideas."

"I'm sure you do."

"Want to hear them?"

"Not at six-thirty in the morning. But yes, eventually."

"Good enough." He pocketed his phone, took her hand. "Come on. Giulia's probably made breakfast and is judging us for our emotional drama."

"Giulia's always judging us for our emotional drama."

"True. But at least there's food."

They found Giulia and Marco in the kitchen, exactly as predicted, with breakfast and judgment in equal measure.

"You look less terrible," Giulia observed.

"Thank you?"

"You're welcome. Eat." She slid a plate toward Sofia—eggs, bread, the kind of simple food that felt like care. "Emma left. Said to tell you she's proud of you for not being an idiot."

"Poetic."

"She's in love. It makes people strange." Giulia turned to David. "You. Did you fix her?"

"Nobody fixes Sofia. She doesn't need fixing."

"Good answer." Giulia smiled. "There's hope for you yet."

Marco raised his coffee cup in a silent toast. David returned it, and Sofia felt something settle in her chest.

This. This was what mattered. Not perfection, but presence. Not having all the answers, but having people who'd help her find them.

"So," Marco said. "What's the plan?"

Sofia looked at David. He looked back at her, waiting.

Partnership, she reminded herself. Building together.

"We accelerate the workshop conversion," Sofia said. "Finish it by Valentine's weekend if possible. Open it for the journalist in

January as 'exclusive preview access.' Use the feature to drive spring bookings." She took a breath. "And we trust that the villa's soul isn't so fragile it can't survive some practical improvements."

David's smile was warm and genuine. "That's a good plan."

"It's your plan. I'm just repeating it."

"You're adapting it. That's not the same—" He stopped himself. "That's different."

"Nice save."

Giulia pointed her wooden spoon at both of them. "If you two are going to be disgustingly functional now, at least do it quietly. I'm trying to cook."

"We're not being disgustingly functional," Sofia protested.

"You're problem-solving together. Making eye contact. Using each other's first names without hostility. It's revolting." But Giulia was smiling. "I'm proud of you. Both of you. Now eat before the eggs get cold."

They ate breakfast together—the four of them, in Giulia's kitchen, planning and arguing and occasionally laughing. Outside, the December morning brightened. Luigi barked at something. The villa hummed with ordinary life.

And for the first time in weeks, Sofia felt something she'd almost forgotten:

Hope.

Not the fragile, desperate kind that broke at the first obstacle. But the sturdy, resilient kind that bent without breaking. The kind that said maybe—just maybe—things could actually work out.

Not perfectly. Not easily.

But work out nonetheless.

Later, Sofia stood on the terrace alone.

She'd called the journalist back. Confirmed the January visit. Offered the workshop as exclusive preview access at premium rate. The journalist had been thrilled—apparently "work in progress" was even more appealing than "finished perfection."

Sofia had also emailed her bank. Requested a meeting to discuss payment options. Not surrender, but negotiation. Not giving up, but asking for help.

It felt terrifying and liberating in equal measure.

"Penny for your thoughts?" David appeared beside her, two cups of tea in hand. He'd learned she preferred tea in the afternoon—one of those small observations that felt significant.

"I'm thinking about my grandmother."

"Yeah?"

"She used to say the villa would test everyone who loved it. Test whether they'd fight for it or just admire it from a distance." Sofia accepted the tea. "I think I finally understand what she meant."

"What's that?"

"Fighting for something doesn't mean refusing all help. It means accepting help from people who see what you're fighting for and want to fight with you." She looked at him. "You see it, don't you? What makes this place special?"

"I do." David's voice was quiet, certain. "It's not the buildings or the view or even Giulia's cooking, though all of those help. It's the feeling that you're allowed to take up space here. That your chaos and messiness and all the parts of yourself you usually edit away are not just tolerated but welcomed."

Sofia felt tears threaten. "How do you know that?"

"Because that's what you've given me. Space to be present instead of perfect. Permission to care about something without calculating its ROI first." He set down his tea, took her hand. "Sofia, you're terrified that success will require you to become someone else. But what if success just means becoming more yourself?"

The question settled into her bones.

All these years, she'd believed that growth meant compromise. That building something sustainable meant sacrificing authenticity. That needing help meant losing herself.

But what if she'd been wrong?

What if growth meant expansion, not reduction?

What if sustainability meant strength, not surrender?

What if partnership meant multiplication, not division?

"I want to try," she said again. "Really try. All of it—the improvements, the partnership, the scary vulnerable thing where I actually let you help me."

"Yeah?"

"Yeah." Sofia smiled. "Fair warning: I'm going to be terrible at it."

"I'm counting on it. Your terrible is my favorite." David kissed her, soft and sure. "We'll figure it out together."

"Together," Sofia repeated, testing the word.

It felt foreign and right in equal measure.

Outside, Christmas lights twinkled in the gathering dusk. The valley below settled into evening, villages glowing like scattered stars. The villa hummed behind them—warm, alive, waiting.

And for the first time in three years, Sofia wasn't afraid of the future.

She was curious about it.

CHAPTER 9: THE TRANSFORMATION

January arrived with unexpected warmth.

Not temperature—the Tuscan winter remained stubbornly cold—but energy. The workshop transformation became a hive of activity. Francesca the architect commanded a crew of local craftsmen with the authority of a general and the vocabulary of a sailor. Marco supervised, ensuring every detail honored the building's history. David coordinated timelines with spreadsheets that somehow made chaos feel manageable.

And Sofia learned, slowly and painfully, to delegate.

"This is torture," she told Giulia one morning, watching workers install the new glass doors from a forced distance.

"This is growth," Giulia corrected, not looking up from her pastry dough. "Also torture. But mostly growth."

The journalist—Catherine Wells, London-based, American accent, sharp eyes that missed nothing—was arriving in three days. The workshop needed to be functional, if not finished. The pressure was extraordinary.

"We're behind schedule," David said, appearing in the kitchen with his ever-present notebook. "The bathroom fixtures arrived wrong. Francesca's threatening to murder someone, possibly me."

"What do you need?" Sofia asked.

"For you to talk her down. She listens to you."

"She doesn't listen to anyone."

"She listens to you more than anyone else." David's smile was quick. "Please? I value my life."

Sofia found Francesca in the workshop, gesticulating wildly at a plumber who looked genuinely afraid.

"This is NOT the fixture I specified! This is builder-grade garbage! I asked for artisan bronze, you bring me Home Depot!"

"Francesca."

"Not now, Sofia. I'm creating art and this man is destroying it with his mediocre fixtures."

"Francesca." Sofia's voice was firmer. "Can we talk? Outside?"

Francesca glared at the plumber one more time, then followed Sofia into the cold morning air.

"He's an idiot."

"He's trying his best with limited information."

"His best is insufficient." Francesca pulled out a cigarette—apparently stress made her revert to old habits—and lit it with shaking hands. "Sofia, I promised you this would be finished by Valentine's. At this rate, we'll be lucky to have running water."

"So we adjust."

"We can't adjust. The journalist arrives Monday. If this room isn't functional, your feature dies."

"Then we make it functional without making it perfect." Sofia leaned against the workshop wall. "What's the minimum viable state? What absolutely needs to work?"

Francesca considered this, taking a long drag. "Bathroom functional. Doors operational. Heating working. Bed in place, even if we haven't built the custom headboard yet."

"So we do that. We make it work for Monday. Then we finish the details after."

"That's not how I operate."

"I know. But it's how I need you to operate right now." Sofia met her eyes. "Francesca, you're brilliant and I trust you completely. But I also trust that a slightly imperfect room that tells a good story is better than a perfect room that doesn't exist yet."

Francesca was quiet for a moment, smoking and thinking.

"Your grandmother would have said the same thing."

"Probably with more swearing."

"Definitely with more swearing." Francesca smiled slightly. "Okay. We prioritize function over finish. The plumber can stay. But I'm not happy about those fixtures."

"Noted."

"And when this is over, we're replacing them with proper bronze."

"Deal."

The next three days blurred into controlled chaos.

Workers arrived at dawn, worked until dusk. David managed logistics with impressive efficiency. Marco supervised craftsmanship with quiet authority. Giulia fed everyone with the dedication of someone who believed food solved all problems—which, Sofia was learning, it often did.

And Sofia learned to trust.

Trust that Francesca knew what she was doing. Trust that David's timelines were realistic. Trust that Marco wouldn't let quality suffer for speed. Trust that the villa could handle transformation without losing its soul.

It was harder than it sounded.

She caught herself hovering. Questioning decisions. Second-guessing tile choices. David finally pulled her aside Thursday afternoon.

"You're doing the thing again."

"What thing?"

"The micromanaging thing disguised as concern." His voice was gentle. "Sofia, we've got this. You don't need to supervise every decision."

"But what if—"

"What if it turns out perfectly because you let experts do what they're good at?" He took her hand. "You hired Francesca because she's brilliant. You trust Marco's judgment. You claim to trust me.

So actually trust us."

"I'm trying."

"Try harder. Go do something else. Anything else."

"Like what?"

"I don't know. Take Luigi for a walk. Call Emma. Bake something with Giulia. Just stop hovering in the workshop radiating anxiety."

Sofia wanted to argue. But he was right.

She was hovering. Radiating anxiety. Making everyone nervous with her nervous energy.

"Fine. I'm leaving."

"Thank you."

"But if something goes wrong—"

"Then we'll fix it. Together. Like partners do." David kissed her forehead. "Go. Trust the process."

Sofia took Luigi for a walk through the olive grove.

The January air was sharp and clean, frost still clinging to shadowed places. Luigi bounded ahead, investigating everything with the enthusiasm of someone who'd never seen trees before, despite living here his entire life.

Her phone rang. The bank.

Sofia's stomach clenched, but she answered.

"Ms. Castellano, this is Roberto from Banca Toscana. We received your request to discuss the February payment."

"Yes. I wanted to explore options for—"

"Actually, I'm calling with good news." His voice was warm. "Based on your recent revenue increases and advance bookings, we're prepared to extend your loan terms. Smaller monthly payments over a longer period. The February payment would be reduced to twelve thousand euros instead of thirty-two."

Sofia stopped walking.

"You're serious?"

"Completely. Your business model is showing significant

improvement. The bank wants to support that growth, not hinder it." Papers rustled on his end. "There's some paperwork, of course. But if you can come in next week, we'll finalize everything."

"I'll be there. Thank you. Roberto, thank you."

"You're welcome, Ms. Castellano. Congratulations on turning things around."

She hung up, stared at her phone, then started laughing.

Not hysterical laughter. Not relieved laughter. Just pure, uncomplicated joy.

The villa wasn't saved yet. But it was survivable. Actually, genuinely survivable.

She called David immediately.

"The bank called."

"And?" His voice was cautious.

"They're reducing the February payment. Twelve thousand instead of thirty-two. They're extending the loan terms."

Silence. Then: "Sofia, that's incredible."

"That's your rate increases and booking strategy working." Her voice cracked. "David, we might actually pull this off."

"We are pulling this off." She could hear his smile. "I knew we would."

"You did not know. You hoped."

"I had data-supported hope. It's more reliable."

Sofia laughed, wiping unexpected tears. "Where are you?"

"Workshop. Watching Francesca terrorize electricians. Want to come celebrate with construction dust and Italian swearing?"

"Desperately."

By Sunday evening, the workshop was functional.

Not perfect—the custom headboard hadn't arrived, some finish work remained, the bronze fixtures were still builder-grade—but functional. Beautiful, even, in its in-between state.

The massive glass doors opened completely, framing the valley view. The stone walls glowed warm in lamplight. The bathroom, while not finished, was operational and surprisingly lovely. The bed—borrowed from storage until the custom one arrived—looked comfortable and inviting.

"It's good," Francesca said, standing in the doorway with arms crossed. "Not perfect. But good."

"It's better than good," Sofia said quietly. "It's real."

David appeared behind them, camera in hand. "Mind if I take some photos? For documentation."

"For Instagram, you mean," Francesca said dryly.

"That too."

They watched him photograph the space—the doors, the view, the interplay of old stone and new glass. He had a good eye, Sofia realized. Not professional, but thoughtful. He captured what mattered instead of what looked pretty.

"He's in love with you," Francesca observed casually.

Sofia's heart stuttered. "What?"

"David. He's in love with you." Francesca said this like she was commenting on the weather. "You can see it in how he photographs this place. He's not documenting a project. He's capturing what you love about it."

"That's... that's not love. That's just good consulting."

"If you say so." Francesca smiled. "Your grandmother used to say love was just paying attention to what someone else cared about. By that definition, David's been in love with you since week one."

She walked away before Sofia could respond.

Sofia stood in the workshop doorway, watching David photograph details she'd never thought to notice. The way afternoon light hit the stone walls. The shadows the olive trees cast through the glass. The specific angle where the valley view was most dramatic.

He was learning the villa's language.

Learning what she loved about it.

Was Francesca right? Was this love?

Sofia didn't know. She'd spent so long believing love meant grand gestures and dramatic declarations that she'd forgotten it could also mean this: quiet attention, persistent showing up, caring about what someone else cared about.

Maybe love wasn't the big moments.

Maybe it was just this.

Catherine Wells arrived Monday morning in a rental car and a cloud of professional efficiency.

She was younger than Sofia expected—early thirties, American accent softened by years abroad, dressed in that specific way Americans dressed when trying to look European and almost succeeding.

"Sofia! Finally!" Catherine's handshake was firm. "I've been dying to see this place. Your photos don't do it justice."

"Thank you for coming."

"Thank you for having me. Can we start with a tour? I want to see everything—the villa, the grounds, the famous workshop everyone's been talking about."

"Everyone's been talking about it?"

"Your architect might have mentioned it to someone who mentioned it to me." Catherine's smile was knowing. "Preview of work-in-progress is very now. People want authenticity, even when that means unfinished edges."

They toured for two hours.

Catherine asked excellent questions, took photos constantly, recorded observations in a voice memo app. She interviewed Giulia about cooking philosophy, Marco about restoration work, David about the business model Sofia was implementing.

"So you're the consultant," Catherine said to David, notebook out.

"I am."

"And you're dating the owner."

David didn't flinch. "I am."

"Conflict of interest?"

"Alignment of interest. I want Villa d'Oro to succeed because it deserves to succeed. That I also care about the owner is secondary."

"Is it secondary?"

"Professionally, yes. Personally, no." David's smile was slight. "Is this on the record?"

"Everything's on the record unless you tell me otherwise."

"Then on the record: helping Sofia save this place is the best work I've done in years. If I happen to be in love with her, that's just excellent timing."

Sofia, standing nearby pretending not to eavesdrop, nearly dropped her coffee cup.

Catherine noticed. "Did you know he was going to say that?"

"No."

"How do you feel about it?"

"Terrified. Thrilled. Confused why we're discussing my relationship status during a professional interview."

"Because authenticity sells." Catherine's expression was kind. "People don't want polished perfection anymore. They want real stories about real people building real things. Your story—struggling villa, divorced owner, consultant who falls for both the place and the person—that's compelling."

"That's not why I agreed to this feature."

"I know. But it's why the feature will resonate." Catherine put away her notebook. "Don't worry. I'm not writing romance journalism. But the emotional truth of what you're building here? That's the story."

That afternoon, Catherine spent two hours in the workshop.

She interviewed Sofia about the conversion decision, the construction process, the balance between preservation and progress. Her questions were incisive, thoughtful, occasionally uncomfortable.

"Why was this so hard for you?" Catherine asked. "Converting unused space into revenue-generating accommodation seems obvious."

Sofia was quiet for a moment, considering her answer.

"Because it felt like admitting I couldn't do this alone," she said finally. "The workshop was Marco's space, but really it represented everything I'd been avoiding—asking for help, making hard choices, accepting that love for something isn't enough to sustain it. You need strategy too."

"And now?"

"Now I understand that strategy and soul aren't mutually exclusive. You can be practical about survival without sacrificing what makes survival worthwhile."

Catherine made notes, nodded. "That's good. Use that exact phrasing when I quote you."

"You're quoting me?"

"Extensively. Your story is the story." Catherine looked around the workshop. "This room is the perfect metaphor—honoring history while building future. Old stone, new glass. Preservation and progress. That's what people want to believe is possible."

"Is it possible?"

"You're proving it is." Catherine smiled. "Sofia, this place is special. Not because it's perfect—it's not. But because it's honest. You're building something real here. That matters more than you think."

That evening, after Catherine had left for her hotel, Sofia found David on the terrace.

Their spot, apparently. Where all significant conversations happened.

"Did you mean it?" she asked.

"Mean what?"

"What you told Catherine. About being in love with me."

David was quiet for a moment, then turned to face her fully.

"Yes."

"That's it? Just yes?"

"What else do you want me to say?" His voice was gentle. "I could give you a speech about when I realized, or how it feels, or why you specifically. But the essential truth is just: yes, I'm in love with you."

Sofia's breath caught.

She'd expected deflection, or qualification, or some hedging statement about timing and complications. Not this simple, devastating certainty.

"I don't know what to do with that," she admitted.

"You don't have to do anything with it. I'm not asking for anything back." David moved closer. "Sofia, I know you're still figuring out how you feel. I know this is fast and complicated and you're scared. That's fine. I can wait."

"For what?"

"For you to catch up." His smile was soft. "I've been living in analysis mode for four years. Feeling something this strongly, this quickly—it's not new for me, it's just the first time I've let myself actually feel it. You're coming at this from the opposite direction. You need time. So take time."

"What if I never catch up?"

"Then we figure out what we are instead of what I hoped we'd be." He took her hand. "But Sofia, I'm not going anywhere. Whether you love me back next week or next year or never—I'm still here. I'm still helping you save this place. Because you matter. The villa matters. This thing we're building together matters."

Tears threatened, unwelcome and insistent.

"That's not fair."

"What's not fair?"

"Being that certain. That patient. That... present." Sofia laughed shakily. "You're supposed to be the emotionally unavailable one. I'm supposed to be the one overwhelming you with feelings."

"I'm full of surprises."

"Apparently."

They stood together in the January evening, the villa glowing behind them, the valley dark and quiet below. Christmas lights still twinkled in the courtyard—Giulia had refused to take them down, declaring that winter needed all the light it could get.

"I think I might be in love with you too," Sofia said quietly. "I'm just... scared to be."

"I know."

"Because the last time I loved someone that much, it destroyed me."

"I know that too." David pulled her closer. "But Sofia, I'm not him. And you're not who you were then. Maybe this time could be different."

"Maybe," Sofia echoed.

It wasn't certainty. But it was possibility.

And for now, that was enough.

CHAPTER 10: THE LIGHT

Valentine's Day arrived with perfect timing and imperfect weather.

Rain fell softly over the valley—not the dramatic Tuscan storms of summer, but gentle February rain that made everything smell like earth and possibility. Inside the workshop-turned-suite, Alessandro and Francesca (the guests, not the architect) didn't seem to mind.

"It's perfect," Francesca said, standing at the glass doors that framed the rain-soaked valley. "Better than perfect. It's real."

Sofia had checked on them three times already. Giulia had physically removed her from the kitchen during breakfast preparation.

"They're fine," Giulia said firmly. "They're happy. They're eating my food and falling in love with each other again. Stop hovering."

"I'm not hovering. I'm attentively hosting."

"You're catastrophizing in formal wear." Giulia pointed at the door. "Out. Go be neurotic somewhere else."

Sofia found David in the library, dressed for tonight's dinner in a way that made her forget why she'd come looking for him.

"You clean up well," she said.

"I contain multitudes." He looked up from his laptop, smiled. "You look beautiful."

"I look anxious."

"Beautifully anxious." He closed the laptop, moved toward her. "Everything's ready. The table's set, the musician is arriving at six,

Giulia's cooking smells like the best decision anyone's ever made. Nothing's going to go wrong."

"You don't know that."

"I know that even if something does go wrong, we'll handle it." He took her hands. "Sofia, breathe. You've done this a hundred times."

"I've never done this. Not like this. Not with everything riding on it."

"Nothing's riding on it. One couple having one dinner isn't make-or-break."

"Catherine's feature published this morning."

David's expression shifted. "It did?"

"Check your phone."

He pulled it out, opened the link Sofia sent him. She watched his face as he read—surprise, then pleasure, then something deeper she couldn't quite name.

"Sofia, this is..."

"I know."

The article was titled "Villa d'Oro: Where Imperfect Becomes Extraordinary." Catherine had written beautifully—about the villa's history, Sofia's grandmother, the workshop transformation, the philosophy of preservation-with-progress. But she'd also written about Sofia. And David. And what they were building together.

"What strikes you about Villa d'Oro isn't its perfection—it's its honesty. Owner Sofia Castellano has spent three years creating a space where people are allowed to be exactly themselves, chaos and all. That she's now learning to extend that same grace to herself, with the help of consultant-turned-partner David Hartley, is perhaps the villa's greatest transformation yet."

David looked up. "Partner."

"She asked if she could use that. I said yes."

"Is that what we are?"

Sofia's heart kicked against her ribs. "I think so. If you want to be."

"I want to be." David set down his phone, cupped her face gently. "Sofia, I got an offer yesterday."

Her stomach dropped. "An offer."

"A consulting contract. Dubai. Six months, excellent money, exactly the kind of high-profile project I'd usually jump at."

"Oh."

"I turned it down."

Sofia's breath caught. "You did?"

"I did." His thumb stroked her cheekbone. "Because I'm not interested in Dubai. I'm not interested in six-month contracts or hotel rooms or proving I'm the best consultant in seventeen countries. I'm interested in this. In you. In what we're building here."

"David—"

"I want to stay, Sofia. Not as a consultant. As a partner. In the business, yes, but also in your life. If you'll have me."

The words landed like a question and an answer simultaneously.

Sofia had spent three years believing she had to choose between the villa and wanting anything for herself. That love meant sacrifice, compromise, becoming smaller to fit someone else's vision.

But David wasn't asking her to be smaller. He was asking to grow alongside her.

"What about your career?" she asked. "Your life? You can't just give up everything for—"

"I'm not giving up anything. I'm choosing something." His voice was firm. "Sofia, I've been running for four years. Different cities, different projects, convincing myself that movement meant progress. But all I've done is move in circles. You're the first person—the first place—that's made me want to stay still long enough to actually build something."

"Even if that something is imperfect and chaotic and occasionally financially terrifying?"

"Especially if that something is imperfect and chaotic and occasionally financially terrifying." He smiled. "I love you. All of you. The chaos, the catastrophizing, the way you apologize for things that aren't your fault. I love that you care so much it physically hurts you sometimes. I love that you're learning to trust people even though it scares you. I love you, Sofia. Completely. Terrifyingly. Without reservation."

Tears spilled over before she could stop them.

"That's not fair," she said shakily. "I was supposed to have a whole speech prepared."

"You can give it later."

"I love you too." The words came out rushed, imperfect. "I'm terrified and I'm probably going to be terrible at this and I'm going to need you to be patient while I figure out how to let someone love me without assuming they'll leave. But I love you. I want you to stay. I want to build this together."

David kissed her—soft and certain and full of promise.

When they pulled apart, he rested his forehead against hers.

"So we're doing this?"

"We're doing this."

"As partners. In business and life."

"As partners," Sofia echoed, testing the word again. It still felt foreign. But increasingly right.

Outside, the rain continued its gentle percussion. Inside, the villa hummed with preparation for tonight's dinner. Somewhere in the kitchen, Giulia was probably creating something extraordinary while muttering about people who fell in love during service hours.

"We should check on dinner preparations," Sofia said.

"We should."

Neither of them moved.

"David?"

"Yeah?"

"Thank you for staying."

His smile was warm and entirely hers. "Thank you for letting me."

The Valentine's dinner was perfect in all the ways that mattered and imperfect in ways that made it better.

The musician arrived twenty minutes late, apologetic and charming. One candle refused to light. The rain intensified halfway through the first course, forcing them to move from the terrace to the library. Luigi stole a piece of Giulia's torta when no one was looking.

And Alessandro and Francesca loved every moment.

"This is what we needed," Alessandro said over wine, his hand finding his wife's. "Not perfection. Just... presence."

Sofia, watching from the doorway, felt something settle in her chest.

This. This was what the villa was for.

Not flawless hospitality or Instagram-perfect moments. But real people having real experiences that reminded them why life was worth showing up for.

Later, after Alessandro and Francesca had retreated to their suite, and the musician had packed up his guitar, and Giulia had gone home muttering about people who let dogs steal dessert, Sofia found David cleaning up in the library.

"You don't have to do that," she said.

"I want to." He looked up, smiled. "Tonight was good."

"Tonight was chaos."

"Tonight was perfect chaos." He set down a wine glass carefully. "Sofia, can I show you something?"

He pulled out his phone, opened his email, handed it to her.

It was a message from Catherine Wells.

Sofia—

The feature went live this morning. Within three hours, your booking system crashed from traffic. My editor just called—it's their most-read travel piece this year.

You have forty-seven booking requests for the next six months. Seventeen specifically requesting the Emma Suite. Eight asking about the workshop/artisan suite.

Whatever you're doing, keep doing it.

Best, Catherine

Sofia read it twice, then looked up at David.

"Forty-seven bookings?"

"Forty-seven. Probably more by now." His expression was complicated—pride and relief and something deeper. "You did it, Sofia. You saved the villa."

"We did it," she corrected. "We saved it together."

"We did."

They stood in the library's warm light, surrounded by books and wine glasses and the remnants of a perfect imperfect evening.

"What happens now?" Sofia asked quietly.

"Now we figure out how to handle success instead of crisis." David pulled her close. "Now we renovate two more rooms. Now we implement the systems that let you enjoy this place instead of drowning in it. Now we build the thing your grandmother dreamed of—a villa that sustains itself while sustaining the people who love it."

"That's a lot of 'nows.'"

"We have time."

"Do we?"

"We have all the time we're willing to give ourselves." He kissed her forehead. "Sofia, the villa's not going anywhere. You're not going anywhere. I'm not going anywhere. We get to build this slowly, properly, sustainably. No more crisis mode. Just consistent, imperfect progress."

The simplicity of this—the ordinary possibility of building something without constant threat of collapse—felt revolutionary.

"I don't know how to do that," Sofia admitted. "The non-crisis thing. I've been in survival mode so long I've forgotten how to just... exist."

"Then we'll learn together." David's smile was gentle. "I'm told I'm very good at creating systems for sustainable operation."

"Very subtle."

"I'm a professional."

Sofia laughed, burying her face in his chest. He smelled like wine and woodsmoke and home.

Home, she realized. That's what David had become. Not a place, but a feeling. The certainty that wherever he was, she could be fully herself.

"Thank you," she said quietly.

"For what?"

"For seeing me. For staying. For being patient while I learned how to let you."

"Always," he said simply.

Three Months Later

Sofia stood in the courtyard, watching Emma and Marco arrive for Sunday lunch.

Spring had transformed the valley—wild flowers everywhere, vines beginning to green, the air warm and full of promise. The villa hummed with life. All six rooms booked solid through June. The workshop suite consistently commanding premium rates. Giulia happily terrorizing a new assistant who was learning that "more garlic" was always the correct answer.

"You look happy," Emma said, hugging her.

"I am happy. It's unsettling."

"Get used to it." Emma pulled back, studied her face. "You look different too. Lighter."

"I'm sleeping more. Catastrophizing less. Delegating occasionally without physical pain."

"Growth looks good on you."

Marco and David were already arguing about something carpentry-related—apparently David had opinions about the new pergola Marco was building. They argued with the easy familiarity of people who genuinely liked each other.

Giulia emerged from the kitchen, arms laden with food.

"Everyone sit. We're eating before this gets cold and I have to kill someone."

They ate in the courtyard—the five of them, plus Luigi hopeful under the table, the spring sun warm overhead. Conversation flowed easily. Marco and Emma were planning a small wedding for September. Giulia was writing a cookbook, though she claimed it was just "organizing recipes" and definitely not a commercial endeavor. David had officially transitioned from consultant to partner—both in business and on paper, with contracts and everything.

"To Sofia," Emma raised her glass. "For saving the villa."

"To David," Sofia corrected. "For helping me save it."

"To both of you," Giulia declared. "For being less stupid than you were in December."

They toasted, laughing, and Sofia felt something she hadn't felt in years:

Peace.

Not the absence of challenge—there would always be challenges. But the presence of support. The certainty that whatever came next, she wouldn't face it alone.

After lunch, David pulled her aside.

"Come with me. I want to show you something."

He led her to the workshop suite—currently empty between guests.

"What are we doing here?" Sofia asked.

"Look." He pointed to the custom headboard that had finally arrived last month. Beautiful walnut, carved with olive branches, exactly as Francesca had designed it.

But there was something new.

A small brass plaque, mounted discreetly on the side:

The Sofia Suite *Where transformation begins*

Sofia's breath caught.

"David—"

"You named the Emma Suite after someone whose story started here," he said quietly. "I thought this room should be yours. Not because you own it, but because your story started here too. The story of coming home. Of learning to take up space. Of choosing to build something sustainable instead of just surviving."

Tears threatened, but Sofia let them come.

"It's perfect."

"It's honest." He took her hand. "Like everything else here. Imperfect and authentic and exactly right."

They stood in the doorway of the suite—sunlight streaming through the glass doors, valley stretching beyond, the villa solid and warm at their backs.

"Thank you," Sofia said. "For all of it. The suite, the systems, the staying. For seeing what I couldn't see in myself."

"You would have seen it eventually."

"Maybe. But it's nicer not having to see it alone."

David kissed her—soft and sure and full of the future they were building together.

Outside, spring continued its patient work. Inside, the villa hummed with life and possibility.

And for the first time since she'd returned here three years ago, Sofia Castellano felt exactly the right size.

Not too much. Not too little.

Just exactly herself.

EPILOGUE
December, One Year Later

The courtyard glowed with Christmas lights.

More than last year, if that was possible. Giulia had somehow acquired seven hundred candles and wasn't apologizing for any of them.

"It's excessive," Sofia said, not meaning it.

"It's Italian," Giulia corrected, arranging yet another grouping. "Also, I heard that British understatement in your voice. David's corrupting you."

"I resent that," David called from across the courtyard, where he was helping Marco hang garlands.

"You're corrupting her," Giulia called back.

"I'm civilizing her."

"Same thing."

Sofia watched them banter, her chest warm with affection. The villa felt different this year. Alive in a new way. Not just surviving but thriving.

They'd renovated two more rooms over the summer. Hired a part-time assistant for Giulia. Implemented booking systems that actually worked. Catherine's feature had spawned three more articles, each bringing new guests, new bookings, new possibilities.

The bank payment? Made early, in full, with money left over.

Her phone buzzed. An email from a new booking request.

She opened it, started laughing.

"What?" David appeared beside her.

"Someone wants to book all six rooms for a week in March. A corporate retreat. They specifically cited the 'authentic imperfection' philosophy in the article."

"Are you going to accept?"

"Absolutely not. Can you imagine? Corporate people everywhere, wanting team-building activities and WiFi guarantees."

"Sofia."

"What?"

"You just turned down approximately fifteen thousand euros because it didn't feel authentic enough."

"Yes. Your point?"

David smiled—warm and proud and completely hers. "My point is you've learned to value the villa's soul over survival. That's growth."

"That's insanity."

"That's the same thing in Italian." Giulia appeared with more candles. "Also, you're right to turn them down. Corporate people have terrible taste in wine."

"This is not a valid business reason," David protested.

"It's the most valid business reason," Sofia and Giulia said in unison.

David held up his hands in surrender. "I'm outnumbered."

"You're outvoted," Giulia corrected. "Democracy."

"This is not how democracy works."

"It is at Villa d'Oro."

They continued arguing, comfortable and familiar, while Sofia watched the evening settle over the valley. The lights twinkled overhead. The air smelled of pine and possibility. Inside, guests were laughing over Giulia's dinner. Luigi was probably destroying something expensive but replaceable.

The villa was alive. Really alive.

And so was she.

"Sofia?" David appeared beside her, holding two glasses of wine. Their ritual, apparently.

"Thank you," she said, accepting the glass.

"For what?"

"For staying. For building this with me. For believing it was possible when I couldn't."

"Always." He clinked his glass against hers. "To Villa d'Oro."

"To imperfect perfection," Sofia added.

"To stubborn Italians who refuse to accept help until they do."

"To British consultants who don't know when to leave."

"To us," David said simply.

"To us," Sofia echoed.

They stood together on the terrace, the villa glowing behind them, the valley dark and star-filled below.

And the light stayed, as it always had.

Just brighter now.

Shared.

Printed in Dunstable, United Kingdom